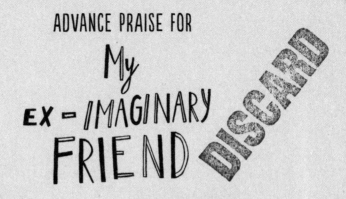

My EX-IMAGINARY FRIEND

JIMMY MATEJEK-MORRIS

CAROLRHODA BOOKS
MINNEAPOLIS

Carolrhoda Books®
An imprint of Lerner Publishing Group, Inc.
241 First Avenue North
Minneapolis, MN 55401 USA

For reading levels and more information, look up this title at www.lernerbooks.com.

Jacket illustration by Tania Rex.

Main body text set in Bembo Std.
Typeface provided by Monotype Typography.

Library of Congress Cataloging-in-Publication Data

Names: Matejek-Morris, Jimmy, 1985– author.
Title: My ex-imaginary friend / by Jimmy Matejek-Morris.
Description: Minneapolis : Carolrhoda Books, [2020] | Audience: Ages 9–13. | Audience: Grades 4–6. | Summary: Told in two voices, eleven-year-old Jack and the imaginary friend he thought he'd outgrown, George, find each other again when Jack's family hits a crisis.
Identifiers: LCCN 2019034440 (print) | LCCN 2019034441 (ebook) | ISBN 9781541596993 | ISBN 9781541599338 (ebook)
Subjects: CYAC: Imaginary playmates—Fiction. | Cousins—Fiction. | Magic—Fiction. | Single-parent families—Fiction. | Depression, Mental—Fiction.
Classification: LCC PZ7.1.M37644 My 2020 (print) | LCC PZ7.1.M37644 (ebook) | DDC [Fic]—dc23

LC record available at https://lccn.loc.gov/2019034440
LC ebook record available at https://lccn.loc.gov/2019034441

Manufactured in the United States of America
1-47805-48245-7/16/2020

TO EVERYONE WHO HAS EVER BELIEVED IN ME.
ESPECIALLY SCOTT.

CHAPTER 1
JACK

"I used to have an imaginary friend, but one day George got tired of sitting around waiting to be imagined, so he left." I immediately regret saying that.

My step-cousins, Jason and Morgan, and Morgan's know-it-all friend whose name I forget stare at me as though I'm the dumbest person in the pizza parlor, and they're probably right.

"Your imaginary friend's name is George," Morgan sneers, nudging her friend. The two of them crack up.

"*Ex*-imaginary friend," I correct, as if that makes all the difference. My face must be as red as the cheap plastic booth we're sitting in, or at least as pink as the bright streaks that pop against Morgan's otherwise jet-black hair.

Mom tries to help: "But now you have *real* friends," she stresses, looking away from her phone for a moment to point out my companions across the table. The condescension dripping in Morgan's laughter begs to differ, and so do I. My step-cousins are both older than I am—Morgan's twelve; Jason is thirteen. They've both always thought they were better than me, even before my mom's sister Rachel married their dad, Dave, to make us officially step-family, and they're both probably right.

"It's fine, Mom." Honestly, I do have some real friends, but they are definitely not at this table. I just don't see much of my school friends in the summer. And I haven't thought about George in almost a year—until a minute ago, when Morgan mentioned his name out of the blue, clearly just to make fun of me. Still, sharing a meal with him would be better than this disaster.

"Eat your pizza," Mom instructs, putting her phone down between us. The cracked screen reveals dozens of unread texts, including some from Aunt Rachel.

"Is that a Siiiiiiix?" Morgan asks in disbelief, adjusting her glasses theatrically as she cringes at Mom's phone.

"No," I snap, "it's a Six *Sssssssss*," as if the S makes all the difference. I think of the cell phone Mom bought me "for emergencies only," and I'm pretty sure it's much less than a Six.

"My dad just bought me the Twelve," Morgan's friend boasts. He pats the pocket of his plaid button-down, his beloved treasure peeking out from the top. "It cost like a thousand bucks, but it's worth it."

"Cool," I say with as little enthusiasm as possible. *My* dad walked out on us nine months ago and never looked back.

"Can we see it?" Morgan asks.

Even the usually silent Jason perks up, rising from his default slouched position and pushing his shaggy hair aside. As my step-cousins pore over the Twelve, I wonder what favor Mom must need from Aunt Rachel that inspired this nightmare of a meal.

George was smart to get out when he could. I take another bite of my pizza and wonder where he might have gone. When I first realized he'd left, Mom said that I made him disappear. It was my fault George was gone. "No one's stopping Greg from coming back but you," she said, as if it were that simple. I could've told her the same thing about Dad, but I didn't.

 ♥ 3 ♠

"It's George," I snapped back instead. Now I can't stop wondering where people go when others stop believing in them. My fourth-grade teacher once tried to tell me the Loch Ness Monster wasn't real, but I've seen the pictures. Nessie lives in Scotland. That fairy from *Peter Pan* almost died when people stopped believing in her, though! So, does that mean that George is trapped somewhere between Scotland, Neverland, and death?

With my next bite, cheese grease dribbles down my chin. I quickly swipe my face with the back of my hand and coolly grin, hoping that nobody's noticed.

Jason smirks. "You . . . uh . . . got something." He points to his teeth. Morgan and her friend cackle.

I wiggle my tongue around to get it out. I have a big space in the middle of my front teeth, like George. He's half-walrus, complete with tan, bumpy skin, the biggest mustache I've ever seen, and enormous gap-teeth tusks. I have no excuse. I usually don't mind having less teeth-space to brush, but I'm mortified as a tiny chunk of olive pops out of my dental food trap onto the table.

"That's disgusting, Jack!" Mom scolds. "Use a napkin."

I tug the paper napkin out from beneath my Coke, which spills over everything.

"MY PHONE!" Morgan's friend cries out, snatching it up as Mom shouts, "OH, JACK!" so everybody in the restaurant can know I messed up.

My jeans and T-shirt are damp. I stare at the embarrassing wet spot on my lap to avoid the disappointed look I've come to know so well: The crooked nose pointed down, nostrils flaring. The tired slate-blue eyes looking right through me. The subtle shake of the head as her fingers rub her temples and then run through her sandy hairstyle-of-the-month, currently chin-length since she chopped her ponytail off in the bathroom yesterday.

She throws her own phone into my hands as she goes to the restroom to get some paper towels. Her bag rattles as she walks away. Everyone in the restaurant is still looking at me.

Suddenly, "You're so Vain" blasts through the air as the screen on Mom's Six lights up with the name *Jerk Face*. I can't believe it. It's him.

"Jerk Face is calling," Morgan's friend snorts. "You gonna get that?"

Breathlessly, I tap *Answer*, bring the phone to my ear, and whisper, "Dad?"

"Jack? Buddy! What's goin' on? Everything okay?"

"Fine," I say, even though things haven't been okay since Mom stopped believing in Dad, and Dad disappeared. He only calls me like once a month, if that, on the landline, and Mom's always hovering beside me to make sure I don't ask what I really want to know.

But she's not here now. "You know I have my own phone now, Dad? For emergencies? Mom got it for me after you left." I wait for him to take the hint and give me his number since Mom always refuses.

"Cool," he says, not taking the bait. Not understanding that his leaving was an emergency.

I push him further. "Where are you, Dad?" Loch Ness? Neverland?

"I'm working—"

"No," I interrupt. "I mean . . ." Why doesn't he understand that he disappeared, and I need to know . . . ? I take a breath, not wanting to scare him away. Carefully, I begin again: "I was just telling my cousins about George. 'Member him?"

Dad lightens up. "Remember him? I love that guy. He's hilarious." George always did tell the best jokes, and Dad was the only one who laughed when

I shared them. Dad continues, "I have coffee with him once a week."

"Wait. What?"

Dad chuckles. "Listen, Jack. I wanted to talk to your mom first, but since you're here, there's something I want to tell you."

Finally, the moment I've been waiting for. "Okay." I press the phone closer to my ear and wait for Dad to tell me exactly where he is and what he's been up to and how much he's missed me and when I can finally see him again.

After an extended pause, he spills out, "I've found someone."

"You mean George?"

"No, Jack. I mean, *someone*. Special."

The words punch me in the gut. My eyes water at the impact. "George was special," I hear myself say.

"Of course he was, Jack. But—"

"*What are you doing on my phone?!*"

I yelp in surprise as Mom yanks the phone from my hands.

"Who are you talking to?" she barks.

"It's Dad," I tell her.

Her whole face contorts with disgust as she speaks into the phone. "What part of 'supervised calls' do you not understand?" Dad says something I can't hear, and Mom fights back: "No. He *was* your son. You walked out on him. On us."

Everyone in the restaurant is looking at me again. Well, everyone except my cousins, who for once are just as embarrassed as I am. I almost take comfort in this fact, until I see that their horrible friend is filming my mom with his Twelve.

Mom continues: "You left and never came back."

Again, my mind flashes to George. He left and never came back. Has he found someone special? "I have to go!" I cry out, pushing past Mom and racing across the wet, sticky, red-and-white tile floor.

"Jack," she calls after me, but it's too late. In a flash, I'm pushing through the door to the great big world beyond. I have to find George. I have to find out where people go when others stop believing in them, or he'll never come back.

It's my fault he's gone.

CHAPTER 2
GEORGE

"Have you seen this person?" the bold red text of the poster asks as I read aloud.

The hand-drawn face grins up at me. I used an orange marker for my skin and blue for my tusks, but it's close enough. I'd recognize me anywhere.

I've made a whole stack of these fliers. I tack one onto a telephone pole before crossing through the gate into the park, a peaceful patch of green amid the bustling gray city streets. A football whizzes by my head, and a speedy girl in a Patriots tee nearly knocks me over as she races past to catch it. Well, peaceful-ish. She looks about Jack's age, ten or so, but he was never this tall or athletic. "Good catch," I call as the ball drops into her arms.

She doesn't even look at me.

I keep trying: "If I could trouble you to look at one of these for just a moment, I'm trying to find out more information about this person. Have you seen him?" I chuckle at how silly that sounds with me standing right here, but in fact, nobody has seen me since—well, since Jack, and I'm getting desperate. I've tried everything:

Chewing with my mouth open.

Talking in a crowded movie theater.

Popping my bubble gum in some guy's face.

Blowing a pretend trumpet in the library.

Heck, I even tried wearing mismatched socks. Once.

No matter what I do, I'm still completely invisible to everyone but me. If these fliers don't work, I don't even know what'll happen to me next.

As I extend the poster in the girl's direction, she flings the football to a friend across the lawn, then races away. My arm droops along with my smile.

A moment later, the whole arm flickers, then completely disappears. Like now you see it, now you don't.

"What the humerus!" I cry out, swatting at my missing right arm with the left one I still have left. This isn't supposed to happen! There's a difference between Invisible and Gone.

My eyes water at the pain I'm sure I should be feeling, but somehow, I feel nothing. My left hand squeezes my right shoulder. There's nothing to feel except an empty T-shirt sleeve flapping in the wind.

The hairs beneath my nose bristle as my last flier takes advantage of the disappearing limb to dance away in the wind. As if a runaway arm wasn't enough of a problem, now I'm littering! I race after the poster, my remaining arm stretched out before me.

The wind carries the poster left, then right, around a tree and finally, up, up, up. My neck tilts back as the sheet of paper climbs through the tall tree's branches and slips into . . . a window?

I gasp when I notice a beautiful tree house resting in the branches. There are rough wooden planks nailed to the side of the tree, stretching from the tree house entrance all the way down to the ground. I'd climb up and retrieve the poster myself if I weren't the teensiest bit terrified of heights. And splinters. And so many things.

"HELP!" I scream for both my missing arm and the discarded flier.

Nearby, two boys are clinging to the jungle gym for dear life, their non-disappeared arms stretched out like rubber bands. They are perhaps the bravest people I have ever seen. They're perfect. I race over. One has dark swoopy hair that kind of looks like Jack's when he first wakes up. The other one, with the ripped jeans, lets go of the bar, falling onto the dirt below.

"Hello, excuse me, my name is George. I don't mean to alarm you, but . . ." I trail off. How can I make them see me? I force out a burp and don't say excuse me. That always used to get Jack's mom's attention when Jack did it. "I could use a hand."

Before the kid in the ripped jeans can answer, the kid with the bed head lets go of the bar and falls to the ground, too. They both start laughing, and I laugh along with them. Yes! Yes, yes, yes! Finally! My lack of manners did the trick!

While I have their attention, I say as quickly as possible, "This is serious. I saw, uh, someone else's litter fly up into that tree, and I thought we could go get it. Keep our park clean, you know?" I suck in a quick breath and add, "Oh and my arm is gone. Hand and everything. So I could use your help."

The kid with bed head turns to the kid with ripped jeans. "Wanna get out of here?" he asks his friend, completely ignoring my question.

"I'll race ya," his pal replies. The two dash across the playground and into the city beyond, leaving me with a much bigger hole than just a lost limb.

I kick the ground. A puff of dirt poofs into the air. "Argh!" I cry out as loudly as I want because nobody can hear me anyway. I don't know why I'm surprised. Jack's the only one who ever heard or saw me before. Why did I think that was going to change now, even if I was perfectly rude?

"Excuse me," I whisper to the universe about that burp as I trudge back to the tree house to retrieve the flier myself. I grab one of the planks of the rickety ladder with my remaining hand, but I don't get any farther than that. Walruses are water people, not tree people.

I attempt to justify myself to no one in particular: "Maybe if I had two arms . . ."

As if the world is listening, my right arm returns. Like, *No big deal. Just a small armcation.*

"Where were you?" I scold it. "Come on. We've got a flier to save." My head tips back, and I take in the full height of the tree. It's got to be at least two hundred feet. My grip on the wooden plank loosens, and I step back to the safety of the grass. Like everything else, this would be a lot easier with a friend.

Jack is so lucky. He found a bunch of friends in school, and before them, he found me.

We were at the zoo. Jack was seven at the time, sitting alone on a bench. "Hello!" I exclaimed as I walked by. When I noticed his frowning face, I slid next to him without waiting for a response. "What're you doing here all alone?"

Jack pointed to a man and a woman arguing not too far away. They were trying to be quiet, but with their swinging arms and angry eyes, I could tell it was not going well.

"You mean the penguins?" I asked, referring to the exhibit behind the angry couple, pretending I didn't notice them. "Did you know that penguins can hold their breath up to five full days when dared?"

Jack's mouth fell open. "Is that true?"

"I dunno. Dare a penguin." I snorted, and Jack snorted with me. Music to my ears.

"I'm Jack," he said, sticking out his hand.

"George," I replied, looking at his hand and slapping it five.

"I like your teeth," Jack said next. What strange small talk, but I wiggled my tongue around to discover two tusks, one on either side of my mouth.

I looked at Jack, who had a similar, though much smaller, gap between his own teeth.

"We're like twins!" I declared.

"I'm not sure if I'd call a walrus my twin," he teased.

"Half-walrus," I corrected him. We both laughed.

The grown-up man who had been fighting approached. "Come on, Jack. Let's go home."

"But Dad, we haven't even seen the monkeys yet," Jack protested.

"Now," his dad insisted.

Jack sighed but pushed himself up off the bench. He looked at me. "You wanna come home with me?" I didn't have to think twice. I popped off the bench, and the rest was history.

That's my earliest memory. Somehow, everything else before I met Jack is a mixed-up rainbow blur. What was I doing at the zoo, and where was I going when I walked past that bench?

Wait a second. The fliers were a good idea, but if I want others to find me, maybe I need to go back to the last place I was found. The place where animals go TO BE SEEN. I need to go to the zoo!

I glance toward the tree house again. "I'll be back," I promise my discarded flier. And if my trip to the zoo is successful, I'll bring a new friend back with me to make that promise come true.

I race toward the street. I stumble when my leg flickers twice—now you see it, now you don't—before returning to normal.

I need to hurry up. I may not have much time.

CHAPTER 3
JACK

My feet fly across the pavement. With each storefront, I find another place where I'm sure George is not. Tats and Taxes. Spin Cycle Gym & Laundromat. Grocerie-Amour. The Law Office of Bernhardt, Beagle, & Wolfmanstein. I'm running out of breath just reading these ridiculous signs. Wow, I've chosen the wrong place to run away, and Mom'll be here any second. George was fun, not boring. Where are the roller coasters? The pirate ships? The jousts?

Stores give way to apartments, which eventually give way to the park. I flop on top of the waist-high stone wall that surrounds the park, hoping to catch my breath, but the wall's scorching hot from the July sun. "Come on, George," I grumble, pushing myself upright. I mean, I created him. How can he be any-where I haven't told him to be? When George was around, I was the decider and he was the follower, but his leaving was definitely not my decision. At least not his leaving forever.

I close my eyes. "Come here, George," I com-mand. My muscles tense when my eyelids squeeze even tighter. I can almost hear my brain waves surge, working their hardest to fix my imagina-tion. Little red and green spots bounce around in front of my eyes. I try to make out George among the shapes, but all I see are tiny dancing donuts. My eyelids pop open; the donuts fade away in the sunlight. When my vision fully returns, I scan the street. Nothing.

So, is he really gone for good? Is Dad? I mean, once you've found someone else, replaced your own kid . . .

I can't even finish the thought. Instead I close my eyes again. "George, get over here." I know it's stupid, but all I can think about is Dad and George sitting at an outdoor Parisian café drinking coffee and eating baguettes, while Dad tells George every-thing about his someone special, and neither one mentions me.

"Ja—"

"—ACK!" I scream as Mom whips me around and wraps her arms around me.

She's sobbing and steaming at the same time. "You son of a—" She gasps for air.

"Mom." I start to sniffle, too.

Her voice immediately softens. "Jack, sweetie, you can't just . . . I was so . . . What did he say to you?"

I don't want to say, or she'll never let me talk to Dad again. "Nothing. I was looking for George."

Her brow scrunches together as she inhales through her nose. "The wallaby?" I nod. Close enough. "Come on, Jack. I have to pay unless we stick your cousins with the bill." A mischievous smile spreads across her face, and I can tell she's actually considering it.

"Mom!" I scold, even though they are the worst. My tone droops as I realize, "They're gonna think I'm so pathetic."

Mom rubs my shoulder. "You're not pathetic, Jack. You're just . . ." She takes another deep breath, struggling to find the right word to describe her pitiful son. "Sensitive," she finally settles on. Sensitive. The polite way to say what I really am.

I swipe the tears from my eyes and run my arm

along my snot-dripping nose. "Mom?" I ask to distract her from what we're both thinking. "What is Morgan's friend's name anyway?"

She shakes her head. "You know, Jacky. I have no freaking idea."

"Not like it matters," I say. "I can't stand him." Tapping my fingers frantically against an imaginary i-thing, I add in a mocking voice, "It costs like a million billion bucks."

Mom smiles. "My phooooooooone," she says, mimicking my tone. We laugh until I let out the loudest, most disgusting, olive-flavored burp, and we crack up even louder. "Ready to go?"

I nod. Suddenly, a flapping paper tacked onto a telephone pole catches my attention. I freeze, and Mom nearly walks right into me. Her purse smacks against my back, and I stumble forward. "Jack! What are you doing?"

"Mom!" I catch myself before falling, run up to the wooden pole, and rip the paper down. The drawing of a fanged boy looks more than a little familiar. *Have you seen this person?* the text reads. Of course I have! My heart is thumping so loudly that I'm sure the sidewalk is bouncing up and down with the vibrations. Look at this guy—it's George! I hold the paper up to my mom. "Somebody else is searching for him, too!"

"Searching for who?" she asks. She takes the paper from me and studies both sides. With a shake of her head, she crinkles it up. "Jack, it's blank." I try to take it back, but before I can, she tosses it into a nearby trash can. "Don't pick up garbage."

"It's not garbage," I snap back. I'm annoyed that she won't listen, but at the same time, I cannot be happier. Mom said the paper was blank. When George was around, she never saw the things he moved, the stuff he made. Only I did. To other people, everything he did was invisible. Which means . . . I reach into the trash and pull out the crumpled paper. "George made this," I announce. "He's alive!" Some light brown liquid drips from the paper. "Eww!" I toss the poster back into the trash can, but its existence is all the proof that I need.

"Jack," she pleads, clearly disgusted. "What are you thinking?"

The next thing I know, I'm back at the pizzeria, washing my hands. When I emerge from the restroom, Mom sighs. "Are we done going through the trash?"

I nod. Even I can't deny how gross that was.

Jason, Morgan, and Morgan's friend stare at me, the freak, as Mom pays the bill. "Are you, uh . . ." Jason begins to ask, before looking down.

"Sensitive," I say, matter-of-factly, as if that explains everything.

"Let's go, folks," Mom says. She softly clasps the back of my neck as we walk out of the restaurant together, like a lioness clutching her cub. I don't remember the last time Mom held me like this. I'm sure part of it is to prevent me from running off and grabbing more garbage, but the grip is gentle, and I don't pull away.

We don't talk as we head to our car parked a few blocks down the street. Certain she's preparing for a lecture, I interrupt the silence with a whisper: "I'm sorry about the trash."

Mom shakes her head and turns to me. "This isn't easy for you, is it, Jacky?"

I'm not sure what she means—Dad leaving, Dad finding *someone special*, the search for George, lunch with my cousins—but no matter what, the answer is no. "It's fine," I lie with a shrug.

She strokes the back of my head, pushing down my cowlick. "You're sweet."

I look up at my mom. Her hair seems lighter, and

her eyes seem dull since Dad left. She keeps saying we should be happier now, but I don't think we are.

She glances over her shoulder at the others, who are trailing behind. With a hint of excitement, she leans in and whispers, "You know what, Jack?"

Honestly, I have no idea what.

She continues: "Let's go find George."

CHAPTER 4
GEORGE

I board the bus behind a gray-haired man with pointy elbows who stoops down and shakes his rear in front of me as he drops his change into the slot. He counts the coins out loud as they plunk against the bottom: "One. Two. Three. Four. Five," then picks up his two large shopping bags and grumbles something before hobbling down the aisle.

As the old man collapses into the nearest open seat, the bus driver glances in my direction. She has curly red hair and brown eyes that look right through me. Remembering that I don't have any money for the fare, I freeze. "Ummm," I begin. Invisible or not, I still feel bad stealing a free ride. An idea hits me. Straightening a pretend tie, I state, "I'm part walrus," extra loud just in case I'm not invisible to the bus security camera. There's got to be a discount for animals going to the zoo, right? Otherwise, how could they afford to get there?

The bus driver closes the door behind me. I stumble down the aisle, struggling to stay standing as the bus pulls forward. I'm on my way.

I slide into an empty seat. A kid covered in freckles sits across the aisle. His slightly-less-freckled mother reads the paper on one side, and on the other, wedged against the window, a gopher-ish creature whispers into his ear. This creature is about my height, wearing an oversized yellow hat, and her face is covered in fur. I try not to stare, but after two or three stops, I realize I am doing nothing but staring, and I think she's staring at me, too. She can see me!

She's not like anyone I've ever seen before, and if I'm not like anyone anyone's ever seen before, are she and I a *we*?

Nervously, I nod to her.

The gopher woman nods back, then glances to the empty seat beside me. One of her eyebrows goes up and the other goes down.

I study the empty seat, too. My fingers run along the bumpy black plastic. I guess we're not exactly the same. She has a friend.

At the next stop, I scurry across the aisle, taking the seat directly behind her.

"Pssst," I pssst at her.

Her head tips back. "Where's your friend?" she whispers over the seat.

"You mean Jack?" I ask, before realizing I'm about to make millions more. "My friendssssssssssss," I correct, "are at the zoo." I feel so cool saying this that I hope she's picturing me in rock-star sunglasses like I am.

The bus rolls to a stop, and the kid, his mom, and the gopher lady rise to get off. The gopher lady pauses to peer down at me beneath the brim of her hat. My left leg disappears before her eyes, then returns exactly as before.

A furry hand flies up to cover her gasp. With wide eyes, she says solemnly, "Find a friend. Fast. Trust me," before following her group off the bus.

"What the hexagon does she know?" I wonder out loud, hoping somebody else can explain what just happened. As expected, nobody does.

As the bus driver calls out the next fifteen stops, I wonder if the disappearing will stop right when I get to the zoo, or if it will keep happening until I've made a friend. I just hope I can find a new friend as easily as I found Jack. Finally, the driver calls out, "Zoo stop!" and I push the panic aside. Here goes nothing.

Bouncing down the aisle and off the bus, I see the grand entrance. Flags with pictures of animals surround the ticket booth. Zebras. Lions. Monkeys. It's great. No walrus, but I'm guessing that we walruses, though remarkably handsome, are incredibly modest. It runs in the family.

I race to the nearest ticket window, hoping that I'll finally be seen now that I'm back at the zoo. "Good afternoon, sir," I say to the man behind the window. "Ticket for one half-walrus, please."

"Next." He gestures to a family behind me, clear permission for me to enter.

I struggle to hold back tears of relief. It's working! "Thank you, sir," I say, before pushing through the turnstile. "Thank you. This means everything." And free admission? You've gotta love these animal discounts!

One hundred penguins and several polar bears later, I've arrived at the prime friend-making location. The glass fence looks over a beautiful teal pool and the loveliest rocks I've ever seen. Seated on those rocks is a trio of walruses, basking in the sun. Besides their luxurious mustaches and their tusks, I don't see much resemblance, but then again, Jack's uncle Dave and step-cousins look pretty different from Jack, and they're still family.

I tap on the glass of the walrus exhibit a few times. One of the walruses swats a fly with her flipper. Or maybe she's waving. My first new friend!

I look at the barrier again. It goes up to my chin. Maybe I could crawl over, but the drop to the water below looks kind of far.

A small plaque stands to one side of the exhibit. *Walrus Facts*, the heading boasts. Well, it's a start.

"The walrus is a member of the Odobenidae family," I read. "Oh my goodness!" My hands leap to my mouth as I gasp. "Ooooh my goodness!" I look left and right and left again to see if anybody else is reading this. If anybody else understands. I can't even believe it. This is amazing! Odobenidae. That must be my last name!

My eyes water as I realize I've never even known my full name before. "George Odobenidae," I say, tipping a pretend hat as I practice introducing myself to others. "Classy."

I make a mental note to get myself a nice bowler hat for the future and continue reading. "Walruses

are most known for their long tusks and ample size."
I shake my belly. It's a little floppy, but I don't know
if I'd say ample. Peering over the glass, I study the
three walruses reclining in the exhibit. "Now *that's*
ample," I say admiringly.

Next on the plaque is a small picture of a bunch
of walruses gathered together on an iceberg. "Walruses spend approximately two-thirds of the time in
water." Wow! I try to do the math to figure out
how much time that means a half-walrus should
be spending in water, but I don't have a calculator,
so instead I keep reading. "Our zoo's walruses are
named Chester, Wendla, and Wanda." What beautiful names. Underneath, there's a labeled photo of
each. Wendla is a rusty color, and Wanda has choc-
olate-chip speckles across her side. Chester is the
amplest of all!

"Chester Odobenidae." When I say it again, a
bell rings. Literally. Perhaps it's the nearby ice cream
cart, but I'm sure there's more to it than that. I think
Chester is my family.

Determined to get closer, I race around the exhibit
to find another entrance. Near the back, there's a
brown door marked *Employees Only*. I'm sure this is
the way, but I don't work here. Yet. Maybe Uncle

Chester can get me a job as an animal artiste or a popcorn seller.

I tap on the Employees Only door for at least five minutes to see if anyone will answer. "Please open up, Uncle Chester!" I cry out. For my final knock, I throw my entire self against the door.

Or I try to, but my hands and arms fade away before making contact. Next my legs disappear, and my eyes, and my fac—

CHAPTER 5
JACK

Mom and I slink along the colorful aisles of the Second Chance to Play toy store, two secret agents on a mission. Mom hums the *Mission Impossible* theme as she grabs my hand and pulls me around the corner into an aisle of floor-to-ceiling "lightly loved" stuffed animals. Other grown-ups stop to stare, but Mom doesn't seem to care.

"Is that him?" Mom whispers with a hopeful sparkle in her voice that I haven't heard since before Dad left.

My eyes follow her gesture to an overstuffed plush lemur that is neither walrusy nor alive. It's not even a wallaby. "He's more humany than that, he wears jeans and T-shirts, and he moves." I try to match her enthusiasm, but my hopes are fading fast.

Mom never saw George before he left. I don't know how she thinks she'll see him now, or why she even wants to.

Mom frowns before bringing an imaginary walkie-talkie to her lips. "The wallaby is still on the run. I repeat. The wallaby is on the run."

My cousins and their friend come around the corner, reluctant participants in our frantic journey all over the city, from the bank (George used to love the free mints) to the community pool (I can't swim, but George was a champ) to this secondhand toy store.

"Are you done kidnapping us yet?" Morgan whines. Nearby parents scan my mother with concerned eyes. A man wearing enough Red Sox merchandise to open a museum takes a step forward.

Blushing, Jason holds up his hand to stop him. "It's okay," he reassures the stranger, which seems to be enough.

Morgan's friend groans. "This place is for babies, and I'm running out of battery."

"You can always borrow my Six," Mom shoots back.

"Aunt Ronnie," Morgan whines, "I thought this was just gonna be pizza."

My mother is not the least bit concerned. "Then consider yourself lucky getting to spend this extra time with Jack."

"Can I just take the 86 bus home?" she begs.

"Oh yeah," Mom replies. "I'm going to let you wander the city on your own. My sister would love that."

"Rach wouldn't mind!"

"Gonna have to eighty-six that idea, sweetie, but thanks for trying." I'm as impressed by Mom's snappy response as I am by Morgan's knowledge of the bus system.

"I'll be by the door," Morgan's friend says. He slinks away. Honestly, I can't blame him. It's fun being kinda silly with Mom, but Second Chance to Play is pure cheese, with yellow walls to match. I avoid making eye contact with the drooping dolls and once-loved plushies that remind me all too much of George, not to mention my dad. When Dad was around, sometimes he'd take me here and warn me, "Don't tell Mom," as he would sneakily buy me a stuffed animal or a small metal car. No such luck with Mom. "We've got to save money," she would always insist. I'm too old for that kind of stuff now anyway.

"Mom," I say, "We should just go home."

She swishes my request away with a flick of her wrist. "Soon," she promises. "But I want you to be happy, Jack, before . . ." She trails off.

"Before what?" I insist.

Leaning in, Mom boops my nose like I'm not almost eleven. "Before I help you find George." Without another word, she leans into a large bin of stuffed animals and begins throwing them every which way, as if George might somehow be buried alive in the middle. Morgan, Jason, and other customers duck to avoid being hit by the soft projectiles.

"Mom," I protest, right before an employee clears his throat and nervously mutters, "Ma'am."

She snaps upright and glares at him. "I am NOT a ma'am," she asserts, threateningly whipping around a plush pink bunny.

He steps back, hands up. "Nobody has to get hurt, ma'am. Madam. Miss."

"Jeez, relax," says Morgan, rolling her eyes. "It's a stuffed bunny." At least she's like this to everyone.

Mom ignores them both, her mind still fixed on the task at hand. "Where did you first meet George?" she asks me.

"I don't know, Mom," I mutter. This is getting

ridiculous. Scheming, I respond with a twinge of hope: "Home?"

"Oh come on, Jack," she protests.

My mind flashes to the moment I did meet George. Mom and Dad were fighting in public again, and as usual, it was all my fault. I shouldn't have spilled my ice cream, and I probably shouldn't have even asked for it in the first place. I had slipped away to a nearby bench to pretend that they were talking about something else, that everything was fine. To un-imagine all the bad stuff that I knew was coming. To— "What're you doing here all alone?" George asked, surprising me as he appeared out of nowhere.

"Come on, Jack, tell me!" Mom insists. People are starting to look at us again.

"The zoo," I reluctantly tell her. "But we really don't have to—"

"Of course! To the zoo!" She hurls the pink bunny at the employee, grabs my arm, and yanks me out the door.

◆

Within twenty minutes, we're parked at the zoo and approaching the ticket booth.

"You swear this is the last stop, Aunt Ronnie?" Even Jason is exhausted.

Mom offers an "Mmm-hmm," as the zoo employee studies our group through a small glass window.

"Twenty dollars for you and fourteen for each of them," the zoo employee says.

Mom clutches her chest and takes an exaggerated step back. "Twenty? Isn't there a discount for wronged single mothers?" She tries to smile.

The attendant looks at her with unmistakable pity and hesitantly repeats the price: "It'll be seventy-six dollars?"

Mom sighs. "You three want to wait in the car?" she asks, looking at Jason, Morgan, and Morgan's friend. I honestly can't tell if she's joking or not.

"Yes!" Morgan's friend practically pleads, before Mom shakes the thought from her head and slips her credit card through the slot.

The zoo employee swipes and hands Mom the card along with five tickets. "Have a great time?" It's more of a question, but maybe we actually will. Mom's trying, and this *is* where I met George. Maybe we're onto something. As soon as we walk through the turnstile, I'm pulling Mom's hand and leading her from one exhibit to the next.

Giraffes. Elephants. Prairie Dogs. Pigeons.

I know it's silly, but I kinda have a good feeling about this, and the closer we get to those walruses, the more excited I get.

Just as we're about to reach the Arctic, the place when I first met George, Mom's phone starts to ring. Fumbling through her purse, she pulls it out and groans. "Jack, I should get this."

"Is it Dad?" I ask.

She slips a five and a few loose ones into my hand and pushes the four of us into the nearest gift shop. "Get yourself something. This'll only take a minute."

I scan the miscellaneous animal figures and keychains and kazoos, before finally settling on a deck of zoo playing cards. These'll be perfect for playing one of the only games I know how to play: solitaire. I peek out the window and see Mom on the phone, getting more agitated by the moment. Whoever it is, they're ruining everything.

I buy the cards. With a quick glance at my cousins, who are buried in their own fancy phones, I slip out of the store.

Mom's back is to me. "No, Rachel," she snaps. "I obviously did not know they had haircuts scheduled, so sue me." It seems Aunt Rachel isn't too thrilled with the "kidnapping" either. "Jeez, sis. I'll get 'em home in like thirty minutes."

I bite my lip, before slipping past the fateful bench where it all began and heading toward the walrus tank. I shove the cards and receipt into my pocket as the handmade flier flashes into my mind. *Have you seen this person?* A smile spreads across my face.

Soon, George. Soon.

CHAPTER 6
GEORGE

The world returns. My nostrils are greeted by the scent of the three 2,000-pound animals who reside somewhere along this damp, winding hallway lined with secret metal doors.

Did I just disappear through the Employees Only door? I thought once people saw me again, the disappearing act would be over. And they're supposed to see me now. I'm at the zoo. That ticket guy told me to enter. Didn't he?

As I try to remember exactly what he said to me, five thousand jingling keys announce the arrival of a zookeeper carrying a bucket filled to the brim with—I sniff the air—what smells like raw fish and clammy water. My stomach grumbles. Who knew a bucket of fish could smell so delicious?

My whiskers prickle when I realize how much trouble I'll be in if I get caught sneaking into the Employees Only section of the zoo. As the zookeeper gets closer, I almost can't decide whether I want to be visible or not. Cautiously, I wave. "Why hello there!" I say. Trying to sound as employee-ish as possible, I add, "Dividends. Financial projections," mimicking Jack's dad. I'm lucky he always used to work at home when he wasn't traveling.

The zookeeper doesn't acknowledge me at all. My heart flickers, deciding for me: being seen and in trouble would be better than this.

When the zookeeper is close enough that I can read her name tag—Josie—I make one more attempt to attract her attention. After twirling my whiskers like a cartoon villain, I dip my hand into the bucket. My fingers wrap around something slimy. "Stop, thief!" I cry as I extract a small clam. It oozes in my open palm.

Josie brushes past, oblivious to the still-one-hundred-percent-invisible criminal.

There's a tiny *splunk* as I toss the clam back into the bucket. I didn't really want to steal. I just wanted to be told not to. "I really thought the zoo would be the answer," I grumble to no one.

"All right, Chester, you ready for your dinner?" Josie asks, and I realize I've overlooked one last possibility. Humans still can't see me—but maybe my fellow walruses can!

"Chester!" I race after her. When we reach a door made of metal bars, Josie sifts through her keys until she's found the right one. With a click, the prison-like door swings open.

I hear the swish of the water against the rocks, and in the distance, I see the three lazy lumps Chester, Wanda, and Wendla. They have the most amazing bulgy eyes, and their whiskers are short disheveled straws sticking out in all directions around their mouths. They're magnificent. And they're my family.

"Who's hungry?" Josie asks. I raise my hand even though I know she's not talking to me. Like a trio of oversized accordions, squishing and stretching, the walruses flop toward us. Josie tosses Wanda a fish.

"Uncle Chester," I cry out, waving both arms and hoping that *he* can see me. I've never tried to meet a walrus before. My legs seem to squish, flop, and stretch as I wobble closer. "It's me! George!"

He grunts, then lifts his head to catch and gobble down one of the clams. Slobber dribbles down his cheek. Did we just make eye contact? I think we did!

I have so many questions, and they pour out of me all at once: "How are Wanda and Wendla related to us? Where do you go to the bathroom? Are you disappearing too? How do you brush your tusks? Do you like working at the zoo? Do they pay well?"

Uncle Chester doesn't answer, but I know you're not supposed to talk with your mouth full of clams, plus I'm pretty sure that whole-walruses don't speak English.

I scan the enclosure as he eats. The water is tropical teal. I crouch down and dip my hand in. Yowza! It's freezing! I yank my hand out and shake it around. Rising to my feet, I notice the crowd. Twenty, maybe thirty people of all ages look down at us from above. A shiver runs along my spine, but it's not from the freezing water. This is . . . it's amazing.

Even though I'm pretty sure none of these people can see me, I wave to the crowd and take a bow. A camera flashes. I pucker my lips and throw back my hips to pose for another cell phone that I dream is taking a picture of me. "You're too kind."

That's when I see him. Pushing between a hipster couple to peer over the glass above.

Goosebumps shoot up my already bumpy arms as my heart drops down toward my ample belly.

"Jack?" I whisper.

Our eyes meet. His pop open, almost as bulgy as Chester's. "George?" I'm sure he shouts, but it's impossible to hear from down here. Jack's mom appears and attempts to pull him away. He fights, but she's bigger and stronger, and the next thing I know, Jack is gone.

"Did you see that?" I ask Wanda, who ignores me like everyone else besides Jack and that gopher lady. "I'm sorry," I say. "It's been great, Uncle Chester, but I have to go. Be back soon."

Within moments, I'm out of the Employees Only section, racing toward the spot where I last saw Jack and his mom. It's nearly closing time, and the crowd heading toward the exit has thickened. "Jack?" I've lost sight of him in the sea of people. "JACK!" I shout this time, my eyes scanning frantically as people almost walk right through me. "Jack's mom?" I call more softly, though I don't expect her to hear me either, since she never did.

There's a break in the crowd, and I see it: the bench where Jack and I first met. It's empty.

My heart is still jumping as I walk over to the bench and sit down. It's warm—freshly used, maybe—but Jack is absolutely not here. I must have made it up. With the excitement of being here, of finding my family, I guess it was wishful thinking. I'd wanted my best friend to be here to share the moment with me.

A stray piece of paper clings to the pavement by my feet. I pick it up hoping for a note from Jack but instead find a receipt. The bluish-purple text says *playing cards*. The paper dissolves as I rub it around in my still-wet hand. Of course Jack's not here.

I trudge back to Uncle Chester's Employees Only door, but I don't disappear through it now that I actually want to. I pound on the door for ten minutes, but nobody answers, and the zoo is about to close.

With nowhere else to go, I hop onto the next bus, hoping to find that gopher lady again, since she's the only one who can see me. The only one who cares. The only one who seems to know what's going on with me and might be able to help.

Unfortunately, there's no gopher lady on this bus, just some high schoolers blasting their music for everyone to hear, and an exhausted woman with a scruffy dog panting on her lap. When the bus reaches its final stop, I switch to the subway to continue my search. But how am I supposed to find her? There must be a billion people in this city.

I should feel worse, but as I think about my day, I can't stop a grin from sneaking onto my face. For the first time in I don't know how long, I was seen. I learned about my family. I met my uncle. It's the backstory that I've been missing my whole life. Now I'm well-rounded. I look at my belly. Some might even say *ample*. Disappearing or not, somehow, I feel ready for the world.

I get off at the Haymarket stop because, I don't know, maybe gophers eat hay? My stomach rumbles as I crawl up the stairs to the street. A mouthful of hay almost sounds good about now. Man, I wish I'd taken some of Uncle Chester's clams for the road.

My stomach blurbles again, and that's when I notice Cone-y Island. The stand's neon pink sign boasts "Thirty-one flavors of ice cream!" and the drawings on the menu board make each flavor look more delicious than the next. Wouldn't mind a quick sundae before my mouth disappears.

I stride up to the window with the confidence of someone with an interesting backstory who deserves to be seen, clear my throat, and politely say to the man behind the counter, "Vanilla, please." Of course, he doesn't hear me, and no burp or mismatched socks or flier or clam heist is going to change that.

My ample belly fades away into thin air, taking my hunger with it.

I bite my lip—which, fortunately, has not vanished yet.

Well. I thought I was ready for the world, but I'm not so sure. A last name and an uncle might not be enough.

CHAPTER 7
JACK

My cousins pop out of the car before it even comes to a complete stop, racing across the front lawn to escape my mom and me. Aunt Rachel greets them at the front door, then scowls at Mom before heading inside and slamming the door behind her.

I'm so mad I almost wish I could go with them. I saw George, and she yanked me away. Dragged me to the car. Told me to sit down and put on my seatbelt before speeding off to drop Morgan's friend at his house, followed by my cousins at theirs. I thought she wanted to help. I should've known she didn't mean it.

The car idles. I can smell the gasoline polluting the air around us. Why aren't we moving? Why aren't we going home?

I glance up at Mom and catch the glimmer of tears in her eyes.

"I try so hard, Jacky." Her voice is broken, the complete opposite of the toy store secret agent. "I'm so sick of failing."

My stomach flutters, and I'm sure she can hear my heart thumping in the silence that follows. Not this again. "No, no, Mom. You didn't fail." I reach across and put my hand on hers, which is clenching the steering wheel. "We succeeded. We found George. Because of you!"

She pulls her hand away and massages her temples. "What did he say to you?"

A tear slips down my cheek, but I keep talking, steady as I can. "He didn't say anything. He was with the walruses—"

"Not George," she interrupts me. "Your father."

Not this. Please not this. My mind flashes back to Mom when Dad first left. The last time she insisted she'd failed. Crying on the couch for days. Sleeping all the time. Not bothering to buy groceries. Forgetting to pick me up from school. This can't happen again. I want to cry but that's not what she needs, so I snort loudly to suck in the tears. Each word is a challenge: "He's busy with work, you know. He said he saw George, too."

Mom runs her fingers through her hair as she takes a deep breath, then smashes her hands against the steering wheel. She's no longer whispering: "Come on, Jack! What did he say that made you run away?"

"It's not important."

Her fist slams on the horn. The horrible blare pierces through the air of Aunt Rachel's usually quiet street. One of the neighbors peeks through their sheer curtains.

"HE SAID HE FOUND SOMEONE ELSE!" I shout. "He's replacing us!"

I start to sob. I should've known the fun Mom who takes me to the toy store and the zoo wouldn't last long. She usually doesn't. I can't let it get further than this though. "But it's okay," I struggle to say. Again, I reach out, rubbing her hand. "We're okay, Mom. Let's go home, and I'll make you a grilled cheese. Just like I used to."

She snorts, almost disgusted. "Back when I was pathetic."

"You're not pathetic," I insist. "You're just . . ." I stumble. What the heck am I supposed to do? George would know the exact right joke to break the tension. "You're just sensitive," I finally say, recalling the word she used to describe me.

"You know that's just another word for pathetic," she snaps. So that's what she really thinks of me. She lets the jab sink in before calmly stating, "I know you'd rather be with him."

"That's not true," I promise. I want them both.

"Then why did you try to run away from me twice today?" she demands.

"We were looking for Geor—"

"Cut the bull, Jack," she snaps. Any hint of sadness has been replaced by annoyance at my stupidity. "You're not seven." Mom gets mad a lot, but I've never gotten used to how much her words can sting. "I know everyone thinks I'm a screw-up."

"Nobody thinks that."

"Your father. Rach. You."

"I don't."

Mom sounds defiant when she says, "But I'm going to show you all."

She's not making any sense, but at least we've gotten past sad. "Show me what?"

"You'll see." She chuckles. The car door unlocks. "Get out, Jacky."

What? Get out of what? Our place is a ten-minute drive away. "This isn't our house."

"Rachel will take much better care of you than I can."

She's kidding, right? Aunt Rachel helped raise those monsters, Jason and Morgan. "What are you talking about, Mom? I wanna be with you."

She unclicks her seatbelt, opens her own door, and comes around to my side of the car. When she opens my door, she insists, "And you will be. But I need a week, you know?"

I don't know.

She undoes my seatbelt and scoops me out onto the lawn. My legs collapse as she releases me, and I fall onto the grass. The cool blades tickle my skin, but I'm not sure if these chills are from the bug-crawling sensation, or the realization that Mom is abandoning me, too.

"I'm sorry, Jack. You're too much. This is all too much, and I need to go." Last time I checked, when you're actually sorry, you don't sound like it's Christmas morning, but Mom is practically giddy.

"Go where?" I ask shakily.

"Away."

She can't even look at me, and I can't ask her the question that's racing around in my mind because I'm afraid she'll tell me exactly what she said about

George: *You're the reason he's gone. You're the reason I'm going.* So that's why she took me to the zoo. Why she pretended to care about George. Why she let me buy the playing cards. To make up for deciding to dump me.

She bends down to kiss my forehead but I pull back. She ruffles my hair, rises, and returns to the car. "Just a week," she promises as the door closes behind her. "I'll be back."

The lock clicks.

I force myself up, my noodle legs wobbling.

I can't believe it. She's leaving me, too. Why does this keep happening? There's a waterfall running down my face, and I'm sniffing and snorting like a pig. I don't understand, so can somebody PLEASE tell me what I've done? "Why does everyone keep leaving me?" I scream.

I smack the side of her car as the engine revs, and she begins to pull away. I run alongside, whacking the front door, then the back door, the trunk, and finally just the air.

The bright red taillights get smaller and smaller, until my mom disappears into the night.

CHAPTER 8
GEORGE

Okay. So my stomach disappeared once. Twice if you count the time all of me did. My right arm, the same. Left arm, not yet.

As I walk away from Cone-y Island, I take inventory of which parts I need to keep an eye on. Well, keep an eye on as long as my eyes don't disappear, too. My hand shoots up and pokes my eyes, one at a time. They fill with water, and I wince. My eyelashes flutter and the sidewalk blurs as I determine that as of right now, I do in fact have two red, swollen, watery eyes. I wonder if the poking made 'em look any bulgier, like Chester's.

I pat my entire face to make sure the rest of me is in place. "Ears. Check. Nose. Check. Whiskers. Ouch!" My fingers recoil from the scratchy hairs.

My whiskers are usually one of my most distinguished features, but not when they get this long. This would happen all the time at Jack's house, but it was never a big deal. Every time Jack noticed my "mustache," as he called it, had gotten too long, the next morning I would wake up to find it shortened. Jack must've cut it in my sleep.

As if I don't have enough to worry about, now it looks like I'm gonna have to find my own way to shorten 'em, and sadly I left the safety scissors at Jack's house. I wonder if Josie trims Uncle Chester's whiskers. I can't imagine him reaching his snout with those flippers.

I peer into the windows of the nearby stores and restaurants until I come across a place called Bath Stuff and Such. The name itself has everything I could possibly need: a bath (because let's be honest, it's been a while), and some stuff (my scissors, I bet)! I don't know what the "and Such" means yet, but I sure hope it's ice cream or a friend.

After three full circles through the revolving door, I find my way inside. My ears are greeted by oldies radio. A row of model beds lines one wall of the store, and there's a large bathtub displayed among the towering rainbow of towels on the other side.

A tiny girl in a cowboy hat nearly walks right into me. She's followed by a slimy green creature with three eyes.

"Excuse me," I apologize to the pair.

"Blagherblah?" the green thing says in response, pausing to examine me.

"You can see me?" I ask.

I scrunch my eyes and tilt my head, checking him out as well.

Just like the gopher lady, he glances to my side. First one side, then the other. "Blunferdee?" he asks, squinting all three eyes and shrugging.

"I'm afraid I don't understand your language," I apologize.

"Come on, Stanley," the little girl says, "bergledorf!"

The fellow oozes after her.

"Stanley? Hey, wait!" I call out after him. "Do you know English? Or Walrusese? Do you know the mysterious gopher lady?"

Neither one turns around. I glance to my lonely side again. How do all the silly-looking ones who can see me know that I'm missing a friend? And if they know it, why don't they stop just a little bit longer and *be* one?

Finding a friend is so much harder than I thought, and after a quick loop through the store, I realize finding scissors isn't much easier. If only I had some help.

The store radio begins singing about a Mr. Postman, and that's when a brilliant idea hits me. I know Jack doesn't want me to go back, but there's absolutely no reason I can't write him a letter! Right? After all, I've learned so much about myself today, I'm sure he would love an update! And once he realizes how interesting I am now, with brand-new adventures and a walrus-based backstory, he might even change his mind about not wanting me around.

I race to the front of the store. The teenage cashier is staring at his phone and mindlessly picking at his teeth. Whatever is stuck in there, it seems serious. I grab a pencil and a sheet of paper by the registers, then dash to one of the display beds. I choose one with an elegant canopy.

"Attention, Bath Stuff and Such shoppers. We will be closing in five minutes," a voice announces. Since I'm invisible, I know no one is going to kick me out if I stay here overnight, so I focus on my paper.

Soon enough, the lights dim. I get lost in my

words. Before I know it, the store is empty, and I'm alone with a completed note for Jack. "Beautiful!" I exclaim, dropping the pencil and blowing a kiss into the air. I fold the letter to slip it into an envelope, before realizing that I don't have a stamp. Or an envelope. "Ugh!" I burst out. "Jack'll never get it now!"

Before I can even frown, I have a great idea! I unfold the letter, cross off Jack's name at the top, replace it with mine, and switch my signature at the bottom with his. It's like my very own instant response from my very own best friend!

Dear ~~Jack,~~ George,

How are you? How is your family? What's new? I've had quite the adventure! You may wonder why I am writing. It is first because I have met my family. Second because I am trying to find a new friend, which is difficult when you're invisible. I am trying so hard, but so far, no luck. How did you do it? ~~I don't mean to alarm you, but I am afraid I may be disapp~~

I miss hanging out with you. I miss the drawer you let me sleep in. I almost miss your peanut-butter-jelly-potato-chip sandwiches, but not quite. Do you like raw clams in fishy water? You should come visit me sometime. I wonder if you will.

Your best friend,
~~George Odobenidae~~ Jack

I read it twice. Okay, four times. I've never gotten any mail before. It's nice to know that Jack's still thinking about me. I stroke my chin as I ponder my letter and all the wonderful things that he said. It looks like he's met some family, too. I wish he'd given me advice on the friend part, though. I am still completely lost. I wonder what he meant about being invisible. It must be a metaphor, or maybe he's trying to make me feel better, like he always used to. I'm glad he's not disappearing, unless he just left it out of his letter the way I deleted it from mine so he wouldn't get upset. After the way things ended, I have to admit I'm a little surprised he wants me to come visit.

Carefully, I tuck the letter under the pillow. I can't wait to read it again later. For now, I think it's time I visit that bathtub on the other side of the store. It's been far too long, and I've got a lot of in-the-water time to make up for if I want to call myself a true walrus and impress Uncle Chester.

I slide off my bed.

Jack's mom's car zips across my mind, cutting through my other thoughts.

I feel dizzy as the colors of the towels surrounding the bathtub seem to fly off the shelves and surround me, like a rainbow tornado.

My legs flicker out. My arms fade away. My . . .

❖

A dim light returns, and I'm at Jack's house, sitting on his unmade bed. I take in the familiar mismatched wooden furniture and white walls smudged with fingerprints. How did I get here?

My hands are shaking. I pat the top of my head, then my cheeks. My toes wiggle inside my sneakers. I'm here. I'm all here. So what's going on? I can teleport? I gulp as I realize what's happened—my longest and most complete disappearance yet.

"Now you see me, now you don't," I say with a nervous laugh. My finger brushes my nose and—hey! Wait a minute. I haven't cut the hairs, and I would have noticed if somebody else had cut them for me, but my whiskers are shorter. I pat them again. Yep. Definitely shorter.

This is—well, it's amazing!

I'm not just part walrus.

I'm part magic!

CHAPTER 9
JACK

Aunt Rachel opens the door to find a sniffling baby on the front steps. "Jack?"

"Can I stay here?" I ask, wiping my nose with my sleeve.

She peers out into the darkness, looking for someone who's not there, and who won't be for at least one week. My heart makes little *sputter-sputter-sputter* sounds that make me want to cry and yell at the same time, but I bite my lip to stay quiet.

"Come in, come in," Rachel says, completely confused. I enter the pristine white living room, my eyes asking what my lips are afraid to say: *What next?*

Her hair is darker than Mom's, and the bags under her eyes are much smaller. She's about to put her hand on my shoulder, but I duck back to close the door behind me before she gets a chance. There's no point. It's not going to help.

"Your mom didn't tell me . . ." Aunt Rachel trails off. "I didn't expect . . ." She can't finish a single sentence, clearly as shocked as I am.

"It's just a week," I state matter-of-factly.

"A week?" Aunt Rachel is flabbergasted.

"A vacation," I mutter, trying to sound nasty, while my insides squish. I wonder why everyone around me needs a vacation from me.

"Of course you can stay here, Jack." Aunt Rachel says as she pushes a wisp of hair from her face and crosses her arms. "Your cousins are on the computer downstairs." She must read the *no thank you* in my eyes because she adds, "Why don't you head on up to Jason's room?" She points up the stairs. "I just need to make a quick phone call."

I trudge upstairs as Aunt Rachel heads to the kitchen, presumably to yell at Mom for dumping me on her.

The second-floor hallway is lined with tons of framed family photos showing my step-cousins doing all sorts of fun things, like standing in front of a roller coaster and sitting on a beautiful Italian fountain. The last picture before I get to Jason's room is a family portrait from Aunt Rachel and Uncle Dave's wedding, almost three years ago. I'm on Dad's shoulders, with Mom by his side, and sandwiched between them is—"George?!" He's a little blurry, but if you close your eyes and turn your head just the right amount, it's him as clear as day.

"What was that, honey?" Aunt Rachel startles me from behind. I whip around. She's holding a cell phone, something in between a Six and a Twelve, which I stare at as if it has all the answers. "Her phone's off," she explains with a frown. "I am so sorry about this, Jack. It seems your mother's going through—"

"I don't have any clothes," I interrupt, not wanting to hear excuses. I don't care what Mom's going through. Doesn't anybody want to know what *I'm* going through?

Aunt Rachel lets out a small sigh. She honestly seems relieved that we don't need to talk about Mom, and I'm relieved that I don't have to listen. "Do you have a key to your place?" she asks.

"Sure," I say. "On my bedroom dresser." I thought we were just going out for pizza today.

"Okay. Well, I'm sure Jason has something you can borrow for now." She beckons me into Jason's room. The walls are military green, although they're hard to see behind dozens of vintage travel posters. A giant cello rests in one corner of the room.

"You can sleep in here. I'll grab the blow-up mattress and see what other clothes I can find in the attic."

I slide onto Jason's bed as she slips into the hallway. There's a lump in my pocket. I pull out my brand-new pack of playing cards. Thanks a lot, Mom.

They drop out of the box and into my hands. The back of each has a picture of a giraffe and says *Wild Cards* in leopard print. I fan them out, face up. The kings are lions, the queens are elephants, and the jacks are crocodiles. The jokers are monkeys, but I put those aside because you don't use those cards in solitaire. I smoosh the cards all over the chocolate-colored comforter, then start matching them up any way I want. In my version of solitaire, there are no rules and you make up the points as you go along, which means you always win, and nobody can call you a cheater. George and I used to play duel-a-taire, which is the same game for two people. He wasn't very good at it, so I always won then, too.

I put the Seven of Clubs on the Five of Hearts.

One week. That's all Mom said she needs, but will it be enough?

I look at the Seven of Clubs and pick it up again. No, that's not right. The Seven has to go on the Three of Spades or it isn't worth anything.

It wasn't enough for Dad.

The Seven of Clubs is still in my hand, but the Three of Spades is nowhere to be seen.

It wasn't enough for George.

I don't get it. I've never lost this game before. I throw the card across the room. It flutters in front of Jason's feet as he enters.

I want to ask him to leave, but it's his room, and when he says, "Hey, Jack," he sounds softer than usual.

There's nothing for me to do but say, "Hi."

"Do you want to . . . play a game . . . or something?"

"You mean on Uncle Dave's team?" I ask, certain he'd never want to play with only me.

Jason bends down to pick up the card I threw and tosses it onto the bed. "Just us this time, buddy."

Buddy? He's up to something. I've never seen Jason play cards that weren't on the phone, and even more suspicious, I've never seen him want to play a game with just me. Aunt Rachel must have set him up to do this. I'm sure playing non-digital cards with his dumber, younger cousin is the last thing in the world he wants to be doing.

When I look up, I notice Aunt Rachel in the doorway with an armful of clothes, her mouth dropped open in surprise. She sneaks back into the hallway. Maybe it wasn't her idea after all. I almost smile, until I remember why I'm here.

"Sure," I tell Jason, with more enthusiasm than I mean to show. "I'll play with you." Remembering George's picture in the hallway, I add, "Do you know how to play duel-a-taire?"

He shakes his head and shuffles the cards with a fancy bridge the way Mom does. "Do you know five-card stud?" he offers as he puts a card face-down in front of each of us, and then a face-up Ace of Clubs for me, and a face-up Four of Hearts for himself. Jason looks at me as if I'm supposed to do something.

I have no idea what's going on, so I try to point out his mistake. "There are only four cards here. Who gets the fifth—you or me?"

Jason almost scoffs, so I guess that was a dumb question.

Before he can comment, I ask my other question, "And where's the stud?"

Jason straightens up. "That would be me," he says as he wiggles his eyebrows up and down and coolly points to himself.

"What am I?"

"You're the bet-ter. You have to make a bet."

A bet? I look at the Ace of Clubs. I need to come up with a really good bet so he doesn't realize how confused I am. I glance up at Jason again before announcing, "I bet you my mom wishes she hadn't left me behind."

Jason bites his lip and squirms in his seat. He doesn't say anything.

Maybe that one bet wasn't good enough. "I bet you my dad wishes that, too."

Jason still doesn't say anything, and he turns his eyes toward a poster of Venice. "I know it stinks." He's almost whispering. Our eyes meet when he adds: "I was five when my mom left. I can't remember the last time we heard from her."

The hair on my arm prickles. I've never really thought about his mom from before Uncle Dave married Aunt Rachel. "I . . ." I have so many questions, but I don't know what to say.

Jason gives me a half-smile as he takes all the cards and shuffles them back into the deck. "Do you want to show me how to play that duel-a-taire game?"

He hands me the deck and I drop it onto the bed, facedown. As I mush the cards around, I make another bet—this one quietly, to myself.

I bet it can't get much more confusing than this.

Suddenly Morgan barges into the room. She looks at me quickly with a "Sup Jack" sort of nod, before turning to Jason, shoving her phone at him. "You've got to see this."

Jason looks at Morgan, at the pile of cards on the bed, and finally at me. "Can't right now. I'm playing duel-a-taire with Jack."

Morgan's eyes widen in disbelief. So do mine.

I just lost another bet.

CHAPTER 10
GEORGE

Being magical is a lot harder than I thought it would be. I've been practicing all night. Once I mastered the classic tricks of whisker-trimming and disappearing, I figured pulling things out of hats or ears or sleeves or other surprising places would be a piece of cake with ice cream, but it isn't. For starters, I still don't have a hat, my ears are kind of small, and my sleeves are short and loose. I did pull some lint out of my belly button, but that was more gross than magic.

I'm sure this is my destiny though. How many times have I said to myself: "Now you see me, now you don't?" With my arms and legs flickering in and out lately, it's all becoming clear. I was freaking out, but it turns out that my body had simply been preparing for my greatest trick. Remembering how I traveled from the store to Jack's bed without even trying, I grin. It was pretty great.

Still, it feels kinda weird being here without Jack. Honestly, after what happened the last time I was here, it feels strange being in his house at all. I shake that memory from my mind because I was clearly mistaken back then. Today I started disappearing, then I thought I saw Jack and a couple hours later, my body magicked me back to Jack's house. If that's not a sign that I'm supposed to be with him, then I don't know what is. He was—no, *is*—my best friend.

I just wish he were home. Before I left, Jack's July bedtime was nine, not . . . I glance at the digital clock . . . six a.m.

At least I've had a lot of time to think about my new life as a magician. With enough practice, I bet I can even magic myself into being seen. Can you imagine?

I've only met one other person with the Magic Gift before, at the fountain right near the Bath Stuff and Such. Jack and I were walking by with his parents when we first saw the Great Macaroni. He wore a beautiful cape made of tarp and decorated with hundreds of white stars, plus the fanciest top hat I've ever seen. Jack's mom tried to push us past, but when he pulled those plastic yellow flowers out of who-knows-where, our feet were glued to the ground. *As if by magic.*

"Wait with him," Jack's mom commanded his dad. "I'll be right back."

Jack almost followed her but stopped when the magician said, "For my next trick, I will need a volunteer from the audience."

I jumped with excitement. "Oh, pick Jack! Jack! My friend Jack! Please! Pick Jack!"

As usual, nobody was paying any attention to me except Jack, who shushed me with a chuckle.

The magician pointed to Jack. "The boy with the big grin on his face."

Jack looked at me uncertainly as he stepped forward. "Go on, pal," his dad encouraged with a gentle push on the back. I stepped forward with him.

"What's your name, son?" the Great Macaroni asked.

"Jack," Jack mumbled shyly.

"Everyone, let's give Jack a great big hand!" the Great Macaroni bellowed.

Jack's dad went, "Way to go, bud!" and pulled out his phone to snap a picture. The rest of the crowd just watched, so excited by the magic that they forgot their manners.

"Now, Jack," the Great Macaroni said as he pulled a deck of cards out of one of his enormous magician sleeves, "I want you to pick a card. Any card." He lowered his voice to sound a bit more mysterious. "But don't let me see which card you choose." The Great Macaroni spread the cards out like a huge fan, and Jack pulled one out: the Six of Diamonds.

After the Great Macaroni put the Six of Diamonds back into the deck and had Jack shuffle the cards, he rubbed his hands back and forth on the deck and closed his eyes. "Now Jack, I want you to picture your card." He paused dramatically. "Are you picturing it?"

"Yes," Jack and I whispered together.

"I'm seeing it," beamed the Great Macaroni, opening his eyes. "Your card is the Queen of Clubs." He flipped over the card on the top of the deck, revealing the Five of Hearts.

"Nope," said Jack.

"I mean, the Two of Hearts," he faltered, flipping over the next card, the King of Spades.

"No," Jack repeated, looking to his dad, then toward the drugstore where his mom was shopping.

"Maybe if I reshuffle . . ." The Great Macaroni sounded nervous, but I knew it was an act. That's when the cards began flying out of his hands like confetti. No. *Like magic.* "Whoops," he said as he bumbled his arms about in the air, frantically trying to catch them.

They landed all over the dirty concrete, some face up and some facedown. The Great Macaroni bent down to pick up the scattered cards. The first card he reached for: the Six of Diamonds. Jack's card! It was so amazing. He had done it! Jack and I clapped excitedly.

The Great Macaroni was very modest, and he blushed to show his gratitude as he scrambled to pick up the rest of the cards. When he stood up, he looked straight at me and winked.

I realize now he must have seen something in me: The Magic Gift. I can't even believe how my past is filling in with these memories. If this doesn't impress a friend, I don't know what will.

The problem is, I've got to practice before I take my show on the road, and I don't think Uncle Chester could pick a card, any card, with his big floppy flippers. Which means I need—

The bedroom door swings open. "Sweet baby

baboons!" I scream, instinctively jumping back and throwing the navy-blue covers over my head. I peek out. Tall-ways, the intruder fills the doorframe. Wide-ways, not really. He's very skinny, wearing a magnificent necktie and a scratchy tweed suit that matches the scruff on his chin. Looks like I'm not the only one who could use the ole whisker-trimming trick. He steps inside. Still shaking, I whisper "Jack's dad?"

He looks around, opens the closet door, and looks around some more. He even gets on his knees to check under the bed. As he's getting up again, he puts his hands on the mattress to hoist himself to his feet. He freezes for a moment as our eyes meet, so I say, "Hi."

He doesn't say anything, but I don't expect him to. It's good to see him, even if he can't see me. I push the covers off me and watch him as he reaches way up into the closet and pulls down Jack's small black duffle bag. He silently begins packing Jack's clothes. That's silly of him. If he's planning on going on another work trip, I imagine his own clothes would fit him much better than Jack's.

After folding three pairs of pants and six or seven shirts, he moves to Jack's drawers. First, he gathers a cell phone and charger. How cool! I wonder when

Jack got those! Several pairs of socks, shorts, and underwear later, he zips the bag closed.

When he takes the bag by the handle and walks out the door, I slide off the bed, leaving the covers in a messy heap. I open Jack's drawers one at a time, to see what's left for Jack when he gets back. I can hear his dad's footsteps go down the hall, stop, then start backtracking. He must have realized that he made a mistake and that those aren't his clothes after all.

"Hello again," I say when he reenters, tipping the bowler hat I wish I had.

He looks at the comforter, bunched up where I left it. He leans forward and peers into it. I don't think he sees what he's looking for, because he frowns. He starts to turn around to leave again but pauses and faces the bed one last time. He clears his throat. "Um. Jack's at his aunt Rachel's house. If you're looking for him," he says to the comforter.

No. Not to the comforter. To me. He's talking to me.

Before I can say anything, he's gone.

I reach into Jack's middle drawer, grab a handful of underwear, and chase Jack's dad out the door.

CHAPTER 11
JACK

"George is here!" Morgan bellows from her room across the hall before hammering down the stairs. Sunlight creeps in through the blinds, and the glow of Jason's phone screen illuminates the ceiling. After staying up late playing cards with Jason, I barely slept all night, yet somehow, it's morning. I couldn't stop thinking about Mom and Dad, and how nobody wants me. How Dad even replaced me.

"What?" The air mattress sounds like two balloons rubbing together as I twist toward Jason in his bed above. I didn't think my cousins knew George. Aren't they kind of old for—

"Yeah," Jason responds, his voice sluggish with either lack of sleep or lack of interest. "Dad said he could come over today."

That's all the confirmation I need. I pop off the bed and follow Morgan downstairs, the pounding of my footsteps matching my heartbeat. I can't believe it. George is here!

"ACK!" I scream as I crash into Uncle Dave at the bend in the stairs and nearly fall over.

"Careful there, pal," he says, slinging a duffle bag over his shoulder and reaching an enormous hand around to catch me. He's a bit of a friendly giant, with a long black beard and a generous belly.

"Sorry, Uncle Dave." I brush past him and don't look up again until I've reached the bottom step. Slowly, I lift my eyes from my bare feet to the bright light coming in through Aunt Rachel's wide-open front door.

And there, standing in the doorway, in his grubby blue jeans and green collared shirt, is that horrible friend of theirs whose name I couldn't remember.

George. So that's his name.

With barely a word, Morgan and impostor-George push past me and head downstairs to play on the computer or whatever new gaming system they have down in the basement now, while I decide that anything in the world would be more fun than that. Anybody need help watching paint dry? Filing tax returns?

I find Aunt Rachel in the kitchen, wearing a burgundy pantsuit and a Star Wars apron, washing pots before she goes off to work. Perfect! "Can I help?" I ask.

She smiles. "Of course." She chooses the biggest pot for herself; I dig around to find the smallest one for me. Every little bit helps, and I'd like to do the littlest bit possible while still seeming helpful.

Silently, I scrub the sponge back and forth against the bottom of my pot, focusing on the crusty yellowish spot that just won't go away.

"Jack," Aunt Rachel begins, using an *I feel sorry for you* voice, which means she's about to bring up Mom.

"Where's she going?" I interrupt, squeezing the sponge. Soapy water oozes from my fist, making its way through the stack of pots and down the drain.

Aunt Rachel swipes her hands on her apron before placing one on my shoulder. It's still wet. "I don't know. She's still not answering my calls but she texted to insist she's fine." Grimy pot-water soaks through my T-shirt, sending a chill down my body. "You have to understand, whatever she said to you, that isn't her."

"It sure sounded like her," I snap, sick of excuses.

"No. What I mean is, your mother has . . . is . . ."
She squats down so we're eye to eye. It's a little eerie
how much her eyes look like Mom's. "Your mom
needs to get help."

"I don't understand."

"Shocking," Morgan taunts. Aunt Rachel and I
flinch as the unexpected eavesdropper barges into
the kitchen, her friend close behind. I wonder how
long they've been listening.

"What she's trying to say," not-my-George says,
"is that your mom is a nutcase." He and Morgan
chuckle together.

My left hand clenches into a fist as my right one
hurls the sponge across the room. It smacks lesser-
George across the face.

"Hey!" he shouts, putting his hands up.

Before I can lunge forward and tackle him, Aunt
Rachel pulls me to her side. "George, you need to
go home," she orders. Her face is red. Everyone
freezes. "*Now.*"

"But I just got here," he argues, dropping his
hands to his sides.

"And now you're leaving!"

"But—"

"*I said go home, George.*"

Morgan shrugs her shoulders innocently. "We only wanted a snack."

"And you," Aunt Rachel says sharply to her, "go to your room."

"But Raaaaaaach," she whines.

"And leave your phone in the basket."

When nobody leaves, I slip between Morgan and impostor-George, through the dining room, up the stairs, down the hall, into Jason's bedroom. The door slams behind me.

Can you believe them? Mom bought them pizza, she took them to the zoo, and now they talk about her like this.

I freeze as I spot the duffle bag Uncle Dave was carrying, now sitting at the end of my mattress. What the—?

I unzip it and find my cell phone and clothes that I'd left back at home.

Are you kidding me?

◆

"Where did you get this?" I demand, barging into Uncle Dave's home office and dropping the duffle bag onto his tiny wooden desk. His big frame looks almost comical hunched over the small furniture, but I am not in the mood to laugh.

His eyes dart over my shoulder, frantically searching for any answer besides the truth. "Your dad . . ." he begins uncertainly.

"*My dad?* He was here?" My mouth drops open. "Why didn't he come in and see me?"

Uncle Dave's smile fades, and he rises to his feet. He towers above me. "You were sleeping," he tries to explain. "He didn't want to wake you, and he had to get to work. He has a trip." Another work trip, another excuse. "He said he'd be back in a few—"

"You could've woken me up," I shout.

He nods. "I know."

"Then why didn't you?" He reaches out, but I step back. "What is wrong with you people? Don't you know what's going on here? Don't you know my mom and dad are gone? My dad found someone special to replace me, and I swear Mom'll be next. Don't you care?"

"Of course we care!" he insists.

"I don't believe you," I snap. "I don't believe any of you anymore."

Uncle Dave reaches out but can't decide whether to pat my head or rub my shoulder or do nothing, so his hand sort of hovers around me, awkwardly stroking the air between us. I'm sobbing. It's pathetic. I hope Morgan and Jason can't hear how *sensitive* I'm being right now. "Do you want me to call him?" Uncle Dave asks softly.

I shake my head. "No." I back away, sniffling. "Give me his number. I'll do it."

◆

I close Jason's door behind me and sift through the things that Dad brought for me. Shirts, pants, socks, underwear, my phone, and my charger. That's it. I scrape the bottom of the bag, hoping I've overlooked an "I miss you Jack" note, but of course there's nothing. You can't miss someone you don't care about.

This is the closest we've been to each other since he left, and he didn't even want to look at me. What is wrong with me? I don't want to think about it right now, so why can't I stop? My lip trembles, and I can feel another waterfall pending.

I unclench my fist and un-crinkle the neon orange sticky note with the ten digits scrawled in Uncle Dave's barely legible handwriting. I tap the number into my phone. It rings and rings and rings. No answer. No surprise. I hang up and turn off the phone. It's clear Dad doesn't want to be with me, so why force him? He can't even give me a—

"Hi Jack."

I jump about five feet in the air, nearly thumping my head against Jason's dresser. There, peeking out of the closet, is a familiar, part-walrus-like figure. I gasp.

He stares back, grinning. "Psst. It's me. George." He steps out of the closet, blinks twice, and clears his throat. "Do you want to see a magic trick?"

CHAPTER 12
GEORGE

Jack's great. When he first saw me, he was so happy he couldn't say anything. Actually, it's been a few seconds, and he still hasn't said anything, but that's okay. He doesn't have to. I know he's glad to see me so I get right to work.

I scoot around the unmoving Jack toward the nightstand beside his cousin's bed. "I'm glad you have these cards," I say, scooping up some fancy-looking animal cards. "I didn't see your dad pack any, so I got nervous."

"You saw my dad?" Jack asks.

"Mm-hm. He told me where you were, and then he drove me here," I say, picking out the two monkey jokers and putting them on Jack's cousin's bed. You don't use jokers for magic tricks. I spread the deck out in front of me and stretch my arms toward Jack. "Pick a card, any card."

"Where's he been?" Jack asks as he reaches out to choose a card, any card. He studies it before handing it back. "Where's my dad been?"

"In your room. Packing your stuff." I shuffle the cards before throwing them all down onto the floor.

"What are you doing?" Jack is finally paying attention to my trick, and it is wonderful.

Bending over, I pull one card out of the mix. "The Queen of Clubs," I announce, before checking my card and seeing I'm right.

Jack's mouth falls open as he murmurs a quiet "Whoa." A tiny tingle runs up my spine. I knew he'd love it! "How did you do that?"

My eyebrows proudly wiggle, as I wag my finger from side to side. "Uh-uh-uh, Jack. A magician never shares his secrets."

"A magician? Since when?"

The word *magician* coming from my best friend's mouth is music to my ears. I was magic before, but now that Jack's here, it feels like I can do anything! I shiver with excitement, and though he doesn't show it, I'm sure Jack is just as thrilled by the possibility.

Maybe one day, I'll even be as amazing as the Great Macaroni.

"Did he say anything else to you?" Jack asks.

"The Great Macaroni?"

"No. My dad!" Jack's talking more loudly now. The excitement of my magic must be too much for him to handle.

"No, not really—Hey, what's that?" Something shines in Jack's ear. Jack looks over his shoulder. "Not behind you. Here!" I pull a brand-new, shiny quarter out of Jack's ear. Reaching to the other ear, I pull out another quarter.

His eyes practically bulge out of his head. Mine do too.

Jack blinks his eyes back to their regular size, but I prefer to keep mine looking as Chester-ish as possible. "George, can you please pay attention for a second?" He sounds serious. "Did my dad tell you when he'd be back from his work trip?"

I shrug. "No." As I try to stuff the quarters into my pocket, I'm shocked to find that it isn't empty. Jack watches in awe as I pull out a long chain of rainbow-colored handkerchiefs. I didn't even know those were in there. It's amazing!

And the best part is, I'm smiling and Jack's

smiling. At least on the inside. On the outside, he's kinda frowny, but I'm sure that's a trick. Jack is very tricky, and this feels like old times. It's great. I twist the colorful handkerchief chain around one of my hands, trying to think of what magic trick I can amaze Jack with next.

Jack watches the cloth wrapping around and around and around. "Dad left, you know. After you did, he just left."

I begin unwinding the handkerchief.

He continues. "Mom's gone, too."

Hold on a second. "What do you mean *gone*?" I ask. Am I not the only one disappearing?

"I'm too much."

"Too much what?" This doesn't make any sense.

Jack shrugs. "Where did you go?" he asks. "I've been hoping you'd come back 'cause I need you to tell me where you were." Looking out the window, he adds, "Where they are."

Wait. So he was looking for me? My whiskers prickle as I realize I was wrong about him wanting me to leave forever. I should have come back sooner! I want to tell him a joke or start a tickle war or do anything just to make him laugh.

"I . . ." I hand him the quarters. That's all

I've got. Really. Jack's question—*Where were you, George?*—flutters around in my head, but my mind is almost completely blank as I search for the answer. There was running away, and then the walruses, but what else? All I can see is a blur of colors, swishing around in a swirl of nothingness. I thought I knew where I was, but somehow the months and months of being away from Jack seem more like a day or two at most; less now-you-see-me, more now-you-don't. So, was I . . . gone? Disappeared?

"Jack?" Jack's cousin's voice sounds outside the door, making Jack and me both jump. I'm so startled I hop back into the closet, and Jack bounces onto his cousin's bed. The door creaks open.

"You okay?" Jason asks.

"Fine," Jack responds innocently.

"Thought I heard talking in here." I peer through the hanging shirts. Jason's hair is longer than I remember, and he looks taller, too.

"Not me." Jack's voice is almost a whimper.

Jason's lips curl into a soft smile. "I guess not." He slowly scans the room. I instinctively step farther back into the closet, although I know he can't see me. "I'll be downstairs if you wanna hang," he finally says.

"K," Jack says. I cross my fingers on his behalf, since I'm pretty sure Jack is lying and would never want to spend time with that guy.

After Jason leaves, I stay in the closet for another minute, trying to sort something out. Before I met Jack, who I was and what I was doing are completely hazy. After I left Jack, things get kinda blurry again. That's when I started disappearing, too. But when I'm with Jack, life is amazing, and I remember it all perfectly. I feel whole. Clearly, I can never leave Jack again, which means I can't let him get bored or annoyed with me this time.

I pop out of the closet again like a George-in-the-box. Jack is startled, almost as if he didn't expect me to return.

"I went to the zoo," I tell Jack. "I met a gopher woman and an alien thing, and get this: I've reconnected with my family."

Jack's face scrunches up with surprise. "Your family?"

I nod. "You've got to meet Uncle Chester. He is a riot." I do an impression of him slurping up a fish, complete with grunts and slobber.

Jack releases a genuine laugh. I've missed that sound so much. It's more joyful than giraffes singing in a choir. I talk as fast as I can, hoping to seem especially interesting and to keep his smile glowing. "Did I ever tell you my last name before?"

He just stares at me with wide eyes.

"Odobenidae," I inform my best friend, tipping the air above my head and wishing I had gotten that hat to perfect the greeting.

"Wow . . . So, do you think my dad was in any of those places? What about your weekly coffee?"

"Coffee?" I want to exclaim *Blech!* but I have never seen a more desperate smile on my best friend's face. He's leaning forward, finally showing me genuine interest. I can't let him down.

I try to picture the *Have you seen this person's father?* poster. His brown crayon eyes peer into my soul. The thing is, I have seen him. I just saw him. And Jack never was very good at finding people right in front of his face. I learned that the hard way. "I don't know where he is now, but I know where he was," I offer. "I'll take you there."

"Really, George?"

I gesture for him to follow me, out the door and down the stairs, hoping that Jack's dad is at the only place I can think he might be, and wishing for Jack's sake that I could be just a little more magical.

CHAPTER 13
JACK

"I'm going to the park," I call over my shoulder after a quick Uncle Dave-mandated lunch. I'm already at the front door, pulling on my shoes.

Uncle Dave stands in the doorway of his office. News radio drones on behind him. I can tell he doesn't want me to go, but the park is right down the street, and Jason and Morgan go alone all the time. After an agonizing pause, he takes a deep breath and says, "Bring your cell phone."

I pat my pocket twice. "Way ahead of you, Uncle Dave."

"Text me updates. Plural. Call me if you need anything. And I want you home before Rachel. Five o'clock."

I look ahead at George, already waiting for me

on the front stoop. He shrugs. "'That should be fine," I say.

"That *will* be fine," Dave says more sternly. "Don't talk to anyone you don't know, and look both ways before . . ."

The rules go on and on. *You're not my father*, I snap, but only in my mind because I'm pretty sure he can still punish me, and it's actually kind of nice to have someone who at least pretends to care. "Yes, sir."

The door closes behind me, cutting George and me free. I shake my head. George and me. I can barely believe it.

"Come on, Jack," he says, hopping up and down and beckoning me to follow him in the complete opposite direction from the park. We're silent for most of the walk, which gives me a chance to catch up to my thoughts: George is back. He's taking me to see Dad. And maybe Mom will be next.

Within fifteen minutes, my heart droops because I know exactly where we're going, and it's not Dad's new place, wherever that is. The houses and trees become increasingly familiar until George freezes and grandly gestures to my house, complete with the yellow door and the missing shingles. "Behold," he says proudly, "the last known location of your father."

"George, I told you he left. He doesn't live here anymore."

"But are you reeeeeeally sure about that?" he asks.

"Yes," I groan.

His smile fades, but only for a moment. "Well, what about your mom?"

I pause. What about her? The last time she acted all defeated like she did in the car, she went directly to . . . My eyes scan to her bedroom window. The lights are off, just like they were back then. "Is she here, George?" I ask, my nerves racing.

"Maaaaaaybe," he says with an uncertainty dipped in optimism.

Not very convincing, but anything's better than Aunt Rachel's house. Only one way to find out. I scoop up a rock from the lawn and roll it around in my hands. I'm going to get in so much trouble for this. With a shrug, I raise my arm to hurl the rock through the living room window.

"No wait, wait wait wait wait!" George calls out, plucking the stone from my fist and tossing it behind me. "There's a key under the tongue of the lawn gnome with the blue suit holding the sleeping rabbit."

I scrunch up my nose and blink.

 93

"I know," he laughs. "It's kinda obvious, but I needed to hide it somewhere just in case."

"Just in case what?"

His eyes scan the grass. "In case you ever wanted me to come back."

It's my turn to check out the lawn in desperate need of mowing, unable to look at him as guilt wraps its arms around me in a suffocating hug. I feel like a monster as I tromp over to the small garden gnome my mom put out years ago.

I crouch down and extract the key beneath his tongue, exactly as George described. Sunlight reflects off the shiny brass as I hold it up, studying it with a squint. I don't remember putting this here, so how did George do it?

I push myself back up to my feet and approach the front door, wondering if this key is even real. My shaky hand glides the key toward the lock.

It fits. With a twist of my wrist, the door swings open. I turn toward George, wanting him to explain but sure he won't understand why I'm confused. We never talked about the fact that the things he created only existed for me, the fact that if he drank a glass of water it stayed full, the fact that when he picked something up only a George-version moved while the real version stayed put. He never noticed then, and he doesn't seem to register that anything is different now.

"Shall we?" he asks, gesturing for me to lead the way.

I step inside. I haven't been home since yesterday before lunch, but it feels like so much longer than that. The old curtains keep out a surprising amount of the afternoon sunlight. There's a staleness in the air. "Mom," I call into the entry. Nothing, but that doesn't mean anything. I stuff the key into my pocket and pound down the hallway, forcing her bedroom door open as I cry out again, "Mom!"

"Whoa," George says as he steps in behind me. A tornado has run through my mother's room. Her drawers are all emptied, and unwanted clothes are thrown everywhere. The only thing that is one-hundred percent definitely not here is my mom.

I take a step forward, stumble over a strappy black heeled shoe that I've never seen my mother wear, and belly-flop onto the bed with a soft thud. Either we've been robbed, or Mom packed in a hurry. And I'm pretty sure nobody would want to steal our junk.

My head sinks farther into her pillow. It still smells like her dollar-store shampoo and the cigarettes she claimed she quit months ago. My nostrils flare, fully absorbing the scent with each deep inhalation, which I realize is creepy as heck, but this is all I've got left. I feel a hand settle onto my foot. Well, this, and George.

I roll over to face my friend, who completely understands. "I'm sorry, Jack," he says. "I know a little bit about disappearing, and she's definitely gone."

"It's only for a week," I assure both George and myself, though truthfully, I'm not so certain.

"Well then, we've got a lot of work to do if we want this place looking spic-and-span before she gets here," he pipes up. "Just look at this mess!"

I shake my head. "It's not my mess. They can clean it up."

"Then what now?"

I think back to all the dumb games George and I used to play, back when nothing else mattered, when nobody was replaced, when everyone was here. All I want is to go back to that life.

As if reading my mind, George whacks the side of my arm and shouts, "You're it!" before dashing out the door and down the hall. It's stupid, and I'm too old for it, but a smile creeps across my face. Finally, someone running away that I know I can catch. I bolt after George, only half-tripping on my mother's shoe as I race out of her bedroom.

◆

Not much is said during dinner but it's not as peaceful as you'd think. Morgan is scowling, and Aunt Rachel and Uncle Dave send each other secret messages with their eyes.

"How was the park?" Aunt Rachel asks me, finally breaking the silence.

"Fine," I say, maybe too quickly. I stuff a forkful of chicken into my mouth before she can ask me for more information. I'm already planning on going back to my house tomorrow as soon as I can escape. George stayed behind, in case Mom or Dad show up in the middle of the night, and I left him my "for emergencies only" number so he can call me if they do.

For dessert, Aunt Rachel scoops out four bowls of vanilla ice cream. Morgan doesn't get one. Instead, she heads up to her room. "No TV or computer, either!" Aunt Rachel warns her from behind as she slowly thunks up the stairs. "And we will be discussing this more later."

The rest of the evening is about as quiet as our dinner. I watch TV with Jason and Uncle Dave. After a while, Aunt Rachel comes in. "Jack, can we talk?"

I'm still not ready to hear more excuses for my mom, so I tell her something I've never said before. "I think I'd like to go to bed now, actually." It's only eight, but today has been a day.

"Tomorrow then," she says.

I nod. Avoiding eye contact with everyone, I call out a generic "Goodnight" meant for the three of them and walk up the stairs.

Before crawling onto my blow-up mattress, I shimmy the pillowcase I swiped from Mom's room onto my pillow. I close my eyes, embraced by Mom's familiar scent and wearing a genuine grin for the first time in days.

CHAPTER 14
GEORGE

As soon as Jack leaves for the night, I flip open his mom's laptop and settle onto the colorful living room sofa. I'd never been allowed to sit on this couch before. Jack usually sat on one end while his mom, at the other end, put her feet on the middle cushion, so I always got stuck sitting on the hardwood floor. It was okay, I guess, as long as you could avoid the splinters.

Jack's dad was usually tucked away at the desk in that little nook in the corner, working. I glance toward the nook and see that it's completely empty now. Jack wasn't kidding. His dad is officially gone.

The computer glows awake on my lap. I open an internet browser and begin my search. "How to use magic to make a disappearing father reappear," I read aloud as I type. Jack wants only one thing, and my magic isn't strong enough to help. Yet. But you can learn anything on the internet.

I scroll through, but all I get are instructional magic videos about how to bend spoons and make coins disappear. I've got to remember those for later, but that's not what I need right now.

I try again: "Use magic to get Jack's dad back." These articles seem to be about characters on TV shows I've never heard of. I wonder if watching any of them would help.

I groan. It's going to be a long night.

I close the laptop and wander over to Jack's dad's office nook. It feels so big now without the furniture that used to be so tightly wedged in there. A desk, cluttered with paperwork. A filing cabinet underneath, always locked. And on the wall, a framed picture of Jack and his dad at a ball game. I remember their matching smiles more than anything. I reach up and rub the hole in the wall where the nail used to be. I'm glad his dad took that picture with him.

Next, I squat where the desk chair used to be and try to get into his dad's head. Tucked away over here, you can't see much of the rest of the living room, except for the corner of the couch where Jack used to sit. I smile, hoping his dad arranged things like that on purpose.

I can't imagine what it would be like sitting here from eight in the morning to five in the evening, and then "five more minutes," "five more minutes," "just five more minutes," until it was time for Jack to go to bed and they didn't get a chance to play catch or checkers or Monopoly or anything at all. I'm sure his dad could see Jack getting sadder and sadder from here.

I don't want to think about that part of the memory, so I dart back to the couch and open the laptop. I look up walrus fun facts and magic tricks that might wow even the Great Macaroni himself for the rest of the night.

Jack escapes from his cousin's house around one-thirty the next day, so eager to talk about his dad. I try to distract him with a million questions: "How was your night? What did you have for breakfast? Did you know that a walrus's tusks can grow up to three feet long? Mine'd almost be touching the floor! Can you imagine? Do you want to see another trick?"

Jack grunts in response, only asking me one question: "Did my parents stop by?"

They didn't, and all I can remember are Jack's sagging smiles as he waited for his dad to play, day after day after day.

I can't bring his dad back, but maybe I don't need to. After all, Jack always had way more fun with me than he did with his dad. I know how to cheer him up. "Knock knock who's there it's a game and we're gonna play 'em all!" I blurt out as quickly as possible. "So what do you wanna do first?" I ask. "Catch, checkers, Monopoly, you name it!"

"George, I don't want—" he tries to argue, but I'm already off to grab everything we'll need.

◆

The next morning, I decide on a new plan: I'll find Jack's mom instead.

When the internet just gives me stories on the Magic of Motherhood, I decide to find her the old-fashioned way. The best way to solve a mystery is to return to the scene of the crime. If the mess she left behind in her bedroom isn't criminal, then I don't know what is.

I study each discarded item of clothing, looking for clues, before I carefully fold and toss it into the closet, hoping that's where everything goes. I never spent a lot of time in Jack's parents' room before, so I'm not exactly sure. Three dresses, five pairs of jeans, an uncountable number of unmentionables because I close my eyes when I pick them up, six socks, two shirts, and one heel later, I still know absolutely nothing, but at least her room looks better.

The only thing left is a bulgy purple purse. I hurl it toward the closet, which isn't my best idea. Loose change and breath mints spill all over the floor, but nothing is quite so loud as the yellow plastic container that rattles as it rolls under the bed.

I stuff everything back into the bag but pause after I've retrieved Jack's mom's pills. *Take 1 tablet by mouth daily*, the label instructs. I scan through the science-y words I'd never be able to pronounce and find a list of warnings. Nothing about disappearing. Darn.

As I examine the bottle in my hands, I remember the one week I did spend in this room, years ago.

Jack was at school. I was doing what I always did when Jack was at school: absolutely nothing. Jack's dad was away on a work trip, which meant I should have had the house to myself, but his mom stayed home sick.

Still in her pajamas and a faded orange robe, she crawled into bed after Jack left and lay there. I waited for her to come out and put on the TV or do something entertaining, but when she didn't emerge by noon, I poked my head in to check on her.

The lights were off. The blinds were drawn. The room was gray. She was on her side with her back to the door. Before I could slip away, I heard the sniffling. Was she . . . crying? I crept farther into the room and crawled onto the edge of her bed. "There, there," I whispered, wrapping my fingers around her warm foot. She gasped, then sniffed again, but more softly.

Unsure what else to do, I held her foot the rest of the day and listened to her crying.

Sometime around two o'clock, she pushed herself up out of bed, wiped her face with a cloth, and took a pill from a bottle just like this one. Minutes later, Jack got home from school, and she was all "Oh sweetie," and "That's great, babe!" Jack never noticed how clammy her skin looked; he never heard the strain in her voice; and I never told him she called in sick that whole week. I held her foot the entire time.

"GEORGE?" I hear Jack's voice downstairs. He's here.

I study the pill bottle one last time and wonder if his mom forgot to take it with her. I stuff it back into her bag, then throw everything into her closet before slamming the bedroom door and leaving that memory behind me.

"Did my parents stop by?" he asks again, and I think he really believes they might.

My mind darts to that yellow plastic bottle, and I kinda believe they *should*.

But the fact is, I'm not their friend, I'm Jack's. He's the only person I can really help. I smile widely. "You go get the ice cream, the pickles, and all the bread you can find. I'll go get the checkers," I say before Jack can stop me.

On Monday, Jack shows up even later. It's got to be at least three o'clock, and he finds me in the backyard on my hands and knees, searching for a bunny that I can use in my magic tricks. Clearly, the only way I'm going to get his parents back is to dive deeper into my magic. I haven't found a hat to pull the rabbit from yet, but one thing at a time.

The knees of my jeans are coated in grass stains. Leaves and tiny twigs have formed a nest in my hair.

"Did my parents stop by?" Jack asks as I rub my hands along my head to shake out the garden debris.

"Not today," I reply.

He frowns. "Great. So what are we going to do then?" His tone is so annoyed, as if I'm the problem. "Tiddlywinks? Duck, Duck, Goose?" He crosses his arms. "Hide-and-seek?"

I stumble backward into a shrub as Jack summons the worst memory of all.

Hide –and–seek.

I waited in that bathroom closet for three days before realizing Jack wasn't even looking. Before understanding he wanted nothing to do with me anymore. Before hiding a key in his front yard and hitting the road.

Jack pulls me from the shrub. "George?" All traces of annoyance are gone from his voice, replaced by concern mixed with a hint of alarm. "You look like you've seen a ghost!"

I have. This house is full of them. Not the *OooooOoooo* spooky kind that would be really fun to talk to while Jack was off suffering at his aunt's place. Jack's house is haunted with awful memories I was hoping to never think about again, but when you're all alone waiting for your best friend to come back and you know you're not who he's really seeking anyway, it's hard not to.

I can't decide if this is better or worse than disappearing, but when I see the worry scribbled across my friend's face, I sigh, suck it up, and say, "You hide first."

CHAPTER 15
JACK

After four days of my successfully avoiding Aunt Rachel's attempts to talk, Jason gives it a try. We're watching TV, just him and me, which is what we do most evenings before and after dinner. His bare feet are propped up on the glass top of the coffee table.

He turns toward me and says, "You know, Jack, your mom, she's, um, going to be okay." He sounds exactly like Aunt Rachel. It's almost like she's told him what to say. I bet she did. Unbelievable.

"Okay," I reply, wondering how to immediately redirect the conversation toward this sitcom that I'm only partially paying attention to.

He continues Aunt Rachel's script: "I know it's really, uh, tough, but it's, it's not about you. Like at all."

"Listen," I interrupt. "Can you just tell Aunt Rachel we had this little chat, and we're all fine now?"

"Rach didn't tell me to say anything," Jason protests.

I almost believe him.

"But I'll stop," he says. I start to relax again, until he continues: "If you tell me where you've been going every day."

My whole body clenches. I let out an involuntary gasp that I hope he doesn't notice. "The park," I lie.

"I went to the park." He tilts his head. "You weren't there."

"You just didn't see me," I insist. My back presses deeper into the plush sofa cushions. I silently will the couch to just eat me right now, but I'm not magic like George. It refuses.

"It's not a very big park," Jason pushes back.

"Did you check the tree house?" I ask.

He shakes his head. "No."

Aha! "Well, I was up there."

"I'll check there tomorrow," he says, clearly not believing me at all.

I flash a gap-toothed grin. "Great."

Later I call my home phone from the landline in the kitchen. George doesn't answer, so I leave a voicemail. "Can't come by tomorrow. Sorry." I hang up before Aunt Rachel or Uncle Dave or anyone can find me using their phone, hoping he gets the message.

◆

I leave for the park a couple hours after Uncle Dave makes us all lunch. When I cross into the gate that surrounds the park, I find a patch of grass right near the entrance where I can sit and wait for Jason to try to bust me. Kids and their parents zip past me, flying kites, catching balls, having fun.

It reminds me of the last few days, running around with George, but these kids seem like they actually want to be here. It's almost hard to watch. I pluck a fistful of grass and roll it around in my fingers. George is trying so hard, but his jokes and games don't make me feel better the way they used to. Even the reason I wanted to find him seems ridiculous now. It's obvious he doesn't know anything about where my parents actually are.

At least Mom'll be home soon. One week. That's all she needed.

"You have a second?" Two beat-up canvas sneakers stand before me, way too big to belong to Jason.

I crane my neck back to find Uncle Dave towering over me.

I sprinkle the blades of grass onto the dirt beside me and rise to my feet. "I was actually just heading home."

"Shame," Uncle Dave says with a shrug. "I was about to take you kids out for ice cream." I peer around Dave, and spot Jason and Morgan waiting at the park entrance. Jason flicks his wrist in a guilt-ridden, halfhearted wave while Morgan almost glances up from her recently-returned phone.

"I guess I have a couple seconds," I say with a smirk.

My twist cone is coated in rainbow sprinkles that are going to be all over this worn red wooden picnic table by the time we're done. Morgan takes a seat by my side, while Jason and Uncle Dave sit across from me.

"So Jack," Uncle Dave begins.

"I don't want to talk about her," I interrupt, hoping I sound only slightly rude.

"Her?" he says, confused. "I wanted to talk about you."

Before I can shut this down, too—because I don't want to talk about *my* feelings *about* her either—he says, "It's great that you're spending so much time outside, but if there's anything else you'd like to do with us . . ." He tips his head toward Jason, then Morgan. ". . . Go to the movies, a bookstore, whatever . . . I'm game. I want to make sure you haven't been getting too bored." He laughs warmly. "Maybe that's impossible though. I know that imagination of yours is—"

"Embarrassing," Morgan jumps in. "Like the time you slid down the bannister at our house pretending you could fly and then you fell into the plant at the bottom." She cackles so loudly that the family at the table beside us turns to stare.

Uncle Dave laughs with his mouth full of vanilla ice cream. It is both disgusting and hilarious. I should be mad, but I kind of laugh along because that *was* pretty funny.

"Or the time you thought you saw an armadillo in a top hat!" Jason snorts. "But it was just a plastic bag."

"Okay. That bag was crawling," I say. "This is not fair. I'm not the only one who's done embarrassing stuff. What about the time *you* fell into the community pool because you were trying to show off to your friends? 'Look how ripped I am guuuuuuuuuuuuuuuys—*SPLASH.*"

We all laugh at this one.

"That was great," Morgan agrees. "Or what about the time you had ice cream all over your face, and you looked like a fool?" she says with a wink to Jason.

"I don't remember that," I have to admit. I take another lick of my ice cream as Jason's arm jumps out and bops the bottom of my cone. It smashes into my face. "You did not just do that!" I cry out, snorting a sprinkle out my nose and holding in a laugh.

I stretch my arm out to do the same to him. He expects it and ducks back, successfully avoiding my boop. Unfortunately for my cousin, he ducks a little too far back, falling off the bench and landing smack on his back. His ice cream splatters all over the front of his shirt.

Uncle Dave is laughing so hard he's practically wheezing. He dips a finger into his own ice cream and reaches to smear it across Morgan's cheek, but she hops off the bench the correct way and races across the parking lot, her precious treat fully intact and her face still clean.

I don't know if any of us except Morgan have gotten to enjoy more than half of our cones, but this is the best meal I've had in a long time. I'm almost happy to be here.

A freezing cold glob smooshes on the back of my neck and oozes down my shirt. I whip around to find Morgan standing behind me, gleefully howling with an ice-cream-coated hand.

Almost happy.

CHAPTER 16
GEORGE

Jack trudges through the front door two days late. I throw my arms around him, not sure whether to cry or yell. "Where have you been?" I demand. "Two days and just one quick voicemail?"

"Is my mom here?" Jack asks.

"I've been worried sick!" I ignore his question, because enough about his mom already. I have picked a card, any card, so many times, and I still cannot magic her back. Can't he even pretend to see how hard I've been trying for like one—

"George." He shakes himself free from my grasp. "Is. She. Here?"

I sigh. "What do you think, Jack?"

His sneakers squeak as he spins toward the door without another word. He's leaving? Already? "No, wait!" I beg. "Please don't go yet, Jack."

He stops but doesn't turn back to face me. My whole body deflates as I realize Jack isn't really here for me. There is only one reason he wanted me to come back at all—to help him find his parents. And in this moment, I understand that as soon as he does, I won't matter anymore. Again.

"A week," he says so softly I have to lean in to hear. "She said a week was all she needed. Today's a week, and she's still not here."

"A week," I echo, not sure how the time slipped by so fast. "Oh crabapples!" I curse. Jack turns to face me, apparently glad we're on the same page. "Uncle Chester must be worried sick about me! I told him I'd be back soon, and then I just disappeared . . ."

"George, can you be serious for like two seconds?"

"I *am* serious," I snap. "You don't just leave your family." I slap my hand over my mouth, realizing that I've said the worst possible thing. "I mean, of course you can do that. Lots of families do. It's perfectly normal." I throw a half-walrus-sized hug around him.

Jack snorts and pushes me off. "Jeez, George. Let's tone it down like five notches. It's okay to say my family is messed up, and that doesn't mean I want yours to be." He presents a generous but strained smile. "Let's call your uncle Chester and tell him how you're doing."

My selfish grin nearly wraps around my entire head as Jack heads for the living room phone.

◆

Using Jack's mom's laptop, we find the number for the zoo, but as it turns out, walruses do not have phones in their habitats and the person who answers is not especially happy to relay our message. "Stop wasting my time, kid," is the exact quote, I believe.

Once Jack has left for the day, I stay on his mom's laptop searching *walrus communication* to find another way to reach Chester. It seems we male walruses have air sacs in our throats to make bell sounds underwater, which we use to communicate with one another.

Aha! I know just what to do!

Within moments, the bathroom tub is full of hot, frothy water. My knees press against the side, and I lean forward, dipping down so my entire head is submerged. I forcefully exhale from my nose, bubbles exploding into the water around me. It sounds more like a whirlpool than bells, but as long as the message gets to Uncle Chester, that's all that matters. I blow again. The especially tiny bubbles tickle my ears.

Once the water has stilled, I listen carefully, and finally I hear it. *Ring-a-ling-a-ling.* I'm so startled my arms slip and I sink farther into the tub. *Dang it*, I think as the loud splash completely blocks the sound, but then it's back: *Ring-a-ling-a-ling.*

This is amazing! Now if only I understood Walrusese. That doesn't stop me from giving it my best shot. "Wring-uh-lingle-ling, Unk-El-Ches-Tor," I try to say in response, but my mouth fills with water. I push myself up, coughing and sputtering. When I can breathe again, the ringing continues, but louder, and coming from the living room.

Oh. It's not Uncle Chester.

It's the phone.

I shake myself dry and snatch up a towel, patting myself off as I race into the living room.

By the time I reach for the receiver, I'm too late. The robotic voice of the answering machine drones, "Hell O. We Can Not Come To The Phone Right

Now. Please Leave Your Name, Phone Num Ber And A Short Mess Age Af Ter The Beep," followed by a brief pause and an earsplitting *BEEEEEEEP*.

"Ronnie, you there?" the voice on the other end asks. I can't believe it. It's him. I shake my head to force any water out of my ears, but even when I'm done, it's still him, as clear as day. "Ronnie, please," Jack's dad begs.

I reach out to lift up the receiver but can't bring myself to interrupt as he continues: "You're not answering your cell. Your mailbox is full. Where the freak are you?" He uses a much ruder word.

There's a long pause. I begin to wonder if he's still there anymore, but sure enough, he goes on: "I never should've given you custody of Jack. You told me it would kill you if you lost him and I believed you, but now you haven't just lost him, you've abandoned him and you—" A muffled voice sounds on the other end, and when he returns, he's calmer, though maybe also crying: "I want my son back, Ronnie, and if you don't call me back, so help me . . ."

Sweat drips down my face. This is an intense message, and somehow all I can think about is what it means for me. I hate that Jack's mom and dad hurt him, that they just left him, but let's be real. If they hadn't left, he never would have found me again. Them not caring about him is what made him care about me. What will Jack do when he hears his father wants him back?

"Let's talk," Jack's dad says, hoping that someone other than me is listening. "Friday at one. Our usual barbecue place. Call me back or don't, but I'll be waiting."

Click.

And with that, everything has changed. I look at the blinking red light and the worn-out blue buttons of the answering machine.

I begin to flicker in and out myself, disappearing for the first time since Jack and I have been reunited. My worst fear is already coming true. Once Jack has his parents back, he won't need me anymore. And then what? I disappear forever?

I can't let that happen.

Next to *Play*, I see the button that will solve this dilemma immediately. *Delete*. My finger reaches forward. Delete. Delete. Delete the message before Jack finds his dad and deletes me for good.

Inches away from the button, I freeze. This isn't right. What would Jack want? What would Jack do?

My head is throbbing; my mind is ringing. I'm pretty sure it's not Uncle Chester calling, but I toss the sopping wet towel onto the answering machine, then race back to the bathtub and stick my fading, flickering head into the now-lukewarm water just in case.

CHAPTER 17
JACK

The sound of Morgan swooning carries from the living room to the stairwell as I head downstairs for breakfast. "I'm in loooooove." What? The giggling that follows draws me in. I find Morgan wrapped in a blanket, kneeling on the couch and facing the end table.

"Stop it," Jason snaps at Morgan, standing with his arms crossed. "It's not funny." Neither one is aware of me standing directly behind them.

"You stop it," Morgan spits back. "I'm your sister, but all you care about anymore is him. Let me have my fun." She reaches over the armrest.

A *beep* sounds, followed by a familiar voice: "Jack. It's me."

"Mom?" I blurt out.

A surprised Morgan's arm slips out from underneath her, and she nearly hits her head on the table, as Jason lurches toward the answering machine. Mom continues. She sounds ecstatic. "Listen, Jack. I have something to tell you—"

"MESSAGE DELETED," the robotic voice says in response to Jason's finger.

Wait.

What?

Deleted? Jason just deleted Mom's message?

"Why did you do that?" I demand.

Jason is momentarily speechless, shame and panic spreading across his face. "She's not coming back yet, Jack. For another week. Maybe two. I didn't want you to hear—"

"The message that was for me? I thought you were my friend."

"Jack, you know I am."

"I'll show you how great a friend I am if *your* mom ever calls." I'm steaming, and I can't stop. "But we both know that's never gonna happen."

Morgan gasps and thrusts the blanket off her shoulders. "Excuse me?" She pops off the couch, about to dive for me. Jason reaches out and grabs her, holding her back, but I don't trust his skinny arms to restrain her for long. I race out of the living room and through the front door. I don't even have any shoes on, and of course, it's pouring, but I can't go back there right now. Mom's still gone, and Jason's conspiring against me.

Each barefoot step across the lawn is met with a disgusting muddy squish. My clothes are drenched within seconds. I wish more than anything that I had shoes, not to mention a raincoat, but I'm not turning back.

Once I hit the sidewalk, things aren't any better. Stretches of slick pavement are interrupted by several inches of water at each crosswalk. I slip again and again along the way, muddying my knees with each stumble. I keep pushing myself up, with so many awful thoughts racing through my mind. Mom wanted to tell me something, and Jason ruined everything. I trusted him. I have literally nobody except George, and I've abandoned him so many times. I'm just like Mom and Dad.

By the time I barge through the front door of my own home, I'm a dripping, shivering mess. My T-shirt is at least ten pounds heavier, the cold fabric desperately clinging to my chest. George pops his head out of the bathroom. He is also inexplicably wet. "George, I am so sorry," I say. I think I'm crying, but with the water running off my hair and down my face, it's hard to be sure.

"It's okay," he assures me. "It's just a little mess. I'll clean it right up."

"No," I correct him. "I mean for leaving you. For forgetting you. For ignoring you. Because that stinks. It really stinks."

The whiskers of George's mustache flutter as he exhales deeply through his nose. He should be telling me not to worry because I'm his best friend and sometimes best friends mess up, so why does he look so conflicted?

After an extended silence, he twitches. It sounds almost involuntary when he finally says, "Not to worry. You're my best friend, Jack." Water splatters across the room when he shakes his head as if trying to toss the words from his lips. "And sometimes best friends mess up. What? No!" His eyes widen as he looks at me. "I mean, yes, of course that's true, Jack. But . . ." He gulps. "I learned a new walrus trick! Lemme show you!" He bolts back toward the bathroom.

I follow him, but I swear I catch a glimpse of a small bunny scurrying across the living room and into the kitchen. I slam on the brakes beside our faded floral sofa.

"What was that?"

"WHAT'S WHAT?! IT'S NOT A VOICE-MAIL FROM YOUR DAD!" George exclaims, before turning around to find me peering into the darkened kitchen.

A what from my who? His whiskers twitch, and his eyes widen.

My neck cranes toward the phone. There's a towel draped over the end table. "What's this doing here?"

"Oh, Jack," George stammers, "it's nothing. Don't touch that. It's not important."

I lift the towel. The red light on the answering machine is flashing. There's a message.

"Uncle Chester called," George is rambling. "Turns out we can send each other phone calls by blowing bubbles underwater."

I tap the *Play* button. "Ronnie, you there?" Dad begins. I freeze. "Ronnie, please."

"My dad called?" I glare at George. "Why did you hide this?"

George shrugs as Dad curses. "The language?"

Dad continues: "I never should've given you custody of Jack. You told me it would kill you if you lost him and I believed you, but now you haven't just lost him, you've abandoned him and you . . . I want my son back, Ronnie, and if you don't call me back, so help me . . ."

I imagine my eyes are crimson as they turn to George, who is shivering. "Wait. My dad wants me? He actually wants to see me. And you knew?" I'm screaming over the end of my dad's message, but I'll play it again a million times later. I hurl the towel across the room, knocking over a lamp that crashes to the floor. George cowers.

A trail of smoke must be spewing from my ears as I take a step forward. "I was wrong about you. Best friend? Pssh. You knew this was all I wanted, and you hid it from me. Why? So we could hang out and play stupid games like we were our own stupid little family, and pretend my actual family wasn't real. Pretend nobody else cared about me besides you. You're not my friend. You're pathetic."

It must be the water dripping in my face or the steam from my ears that makes George seem to flicker in and out right before my eyes. "Jack, I have a trick that'll cheer you right up."

"ENOUGH WITH THE MAGIC!" I scream. "You are NOT a magician. I never made you that way."

George's eyes are wide and pleading. "Maybe it was my family who made me that—"

"Enough with your stupid fantasies, George. Guess what? Your family: also not real. Because you. Are. Not—"

"Jack!" George interrupts me, pointing to the door.

I follow his gesture to find a sopping Jason standing in the doorway, concern scrawled across his wobbly lips and slanted brows. Oh crap.

"Get out!" I yell at him instinctively. "Just leave me alone!"

Jason holds both hands up, muttering, "Sorry. Sorry, Jack," and quickly exits.

"Fantastic," I grumble. If he tells Aunt Rachel and Uncle Dave where I've been, they'll kill me. "Now look what you've done," I snap at George as if it's somehow his fault. Racing back out into the storm, I call out, "Jason, wait!"

He's gone.

CHAPTER 18
GEORGE

've gotta get out of here. I run toward the front door, parts of me blinking in and out every few steps. Jack doesn't need me. He doesn't even like me. I've ruined everything.

My leg fades away and the rest of me collapses onto the floor.

And the things he said to me. I don't know how, but they changed me. When he said I didn't know magic, I swear I could hear the sound of my magic flying right out of me, fluttering like cards in the wind. And what he said about Uncle Lester. Hester? What's her name? Whose? I rub my head hoping to stir my memory but there's no point. My family's gone, too.

I think back to the mysterious gopher lady who

urged me to get a friend. "I had one," I whisper to her, puffing out my cheeks and *pbbffting* in case gophers can hear walrus bells across space. "But I've ruined everything."

Nobody's ever spoken to me the way Jack just did, but then again, nobody ever spoke to me at all before Jack.

"Now you've done it, George." I would kick myself, if only my leg weren't currently MIA. "You are such an idiot," I tell myself instead. "You should've just told him and we could've found his dad together. But you didn't, and now you can't stop disapp—"

CHAPTER 19
JACK

Jason must have taken his bike, because he's nowhere to be found. I run all the way back to Aunt Rachel's, my bare feet almost numb to the mud and water at this point.

Out of breath, I push through the front door. "Jason," I hiss, looking up the stairs. His bedroom light seems to be on, so I bolt up after him. A trail of brown footsteps follows me, blemishing the usually spotless floors. Great. Because I'm not in enough trouble. I pop into the bedroom, vowing to get a towel and scrub up the mess after a quick word with my cousin. "Jason, you can't tell Aunt—"

"Tell me what?" Aunt Rachel says, sitting on my air mattress, wringing Mom's pillow case around in her hands. She's shaking. "You want to tell me where you got this?"

Oh shoot.

◆

I perch on the edge of the bathtub with my feet inside as it fills with water. Aunt Rachel stands behind me, squeezing a bottle of soap that makes fart sounds as it shoots pink bubbly liquid into the tub.

"Scrub," she commands in a no-nonsense voice, turning off the tap and handing me a scratchy teal washcloth. I get started. She watches like a hawk, both of us unsure what to say next. The water swishes back and forth as I scrub mud, grass, and even some blood from my heels to my knees. "Not even any shoes, Jack?" she sighs, starting with the least loaded matter at hand.

"I had to get outta here fast," I try to explain. "Mom left me a message, and Jason just deleted it!"

Aunt Rachel nods. "I know."

"So you heard it too?" I frown at this new betrayal, but after Mom, Jason, and George, I can't say I'm surprised. "You knew she wasn't coming back, and you said nothing?"

Aunt Rachel inhales deeply. "Your mother *will* be back," she insists. I catch a sense of desperation in her voice, as if me staying here forever would be the worst thing imaginable, and I have to agree. Thank God for Dad's message. "And when she does get back," Aunt Rachel continues, "she's going to need you more than you know."

"She has a funny way of showing how much she needs me," I fight back, tossing the washcloth into the tub, lifting my legs, and spinning around to face Rachel. My feet drip on the white floor. Rachel hands me a giant fluffy towel. "Thanks," I mumble, quickly wiping my legs dry.

There's a tap on the open bathroom door, and Uncle Dave pokes his head in. "Everything okay in here?" he asks softly.

I say "Yeah," as Aunt Rachel shakes her head no.

Dave crosses his arms and leans against the doorway, his imposing body blocking any chance of escape. He begins his portion of the interrogation: "Should we discuss how you told me you'd be at the park, a block down the street, and I trusted you, Jack, only to find you've been trekking to your house alone every day for the past week?"

"I wasn't alone. George was with me."

Aunt Rachel scrunches her brow in disbelief. "George? I thought you hated him."

"I do now," I agree just as I realize she's probably talking about Morgan's horrible friend, not mine. Ah well. I hate them both. "Did you know my dad called? He wants me. He's always wanted me. And my mom said no. I hate her. She's insane!"

"Stop it!" Aunt Rachel snaps. Her words echo across the tile, and I nearly fall back into the tub in surprise.

In a softer tone, she goes on, "That word is not okay, Jack. Your mother is not insane. She's just . . ." Once again, she trails off like she always does when she's trying to talk about Mom, but this time I catch a tear streaming down her cheek. I wait for her to say *sensitive*. Instead, Aunt Rachel shocks me as she says, "She's not well."

My back stiffens. "You mean she's sick?"

Rachel flinches a little but nods. "Yes." Each word that follows is slow and deliberate, like she's terrified of saying the wrong thing. "She feels things, emotions, differently than us. More extreme. And when those emotions take control . . ." Rachel looks toward Uncle Dave, like she's unsure if she should say more, but I already know what happens when they do. I end up here. She finally continues, "I thought she had things in check this time."

"This time?" I can't even believe it. "You mean she's done this before? You all knew this could happen? She knew? And nobody said anything?"

"She was taking her meds. She was doing better," Aunt Rachel says defensively, glancing down at her chipped fingernails before adding, "At least I thought she was."

"This is crazy."

There's a *THWACK* as Aunt Rachel's foot kicks the cabinet behind her, startling a pathetic sniffle-snort out of me. "Use that word again, and I swear—"

"What your aunt means," Dave interrupts in a struggle to change the tone, "is there are wrong ways to talk about this, and not talking at all is one of the wrong-est. We should have been more open with you, Jack." He's too late, though. For something to make Aunt Rachel speak like that—like Mom—I know things are way worse than I could ever imagine.

In a hushed tone, her calmness restored, Rachel continues, "When your mom comes back, if it's like last time, she's not going to be the same for a while. She might not be the way you feel you need her to be. But you need to know that we are all here for you and that she will get better. Everything will be okay again."

"Okay," I mutter, even though things haven't felt okay in years.

Aunt Rachel scoops the towel off the floor and tosses it into the sink behind her, then reaches past me and flicks the drain lever. Slurpy sucking sounds punctuate the painful seriousness of this moment.

"You don't need to worry about me," I promise Aunt Rachel, with as reassuring a look as I can muster, despite my racing mind. Mom is sick. And Dad wants to be with me. Does he know Mom is sick? Will he come back if he finds out how much she needs our help?

I look up to my aunt and uncle, who are waiting for me to say more. Rachel's hair seems disheveled, and I realize I have the same effect on everyone. "I'm sorry," I say, before finally standing and pulling Aunt Rachel into a hug, because that's all I've got. *I'm sorry I scared you. I'm sorry I ruined your floors. Sorry my mom has you all worked up. That she has for years.* I squeeze Aunt Rachel a little tighter because I know what I have to do next.

I'm sorry I can't stay.

CHAPTER 20
GEORGE

The floor beneath me seems to be made of rainbow Jell-O. It wobbles and threatens to collapse with each step. I take bigger, bouncier strides, as I desperately search for more solid ground. Instead, I find a thick air that seems to hold me up longer and farther with each bounce. I'm floating, almost flying.

And I thought I was magic before. Shows what Jack knows!

Rather than the usual light blue sky I've come to know, the atmosphere here is a swirl of rainbow sherbet. "Something's wrong with the gravity," I announce to anyone who will listen.

Three mice—one brown, one gray, one purple—scurry past me along the gelatinous ground, their tiny feet making dents in its fragile surface. "It's fine," one replies, with a much gruffer voice than I'd expect from such a small creature.

"Excuse me. Where are we?" I chase after them as I scan the horizon. Whimsical buildings that look like cartoon drawings dot the street. Some have faces. Dozens of curious creatures poke their heads out of windows while others float or bounce along the sidewalk.

An enormous, four-headed turquoise monster wearing a red striped button-down shirt strolls past, singing in harmony—a barbershop quartet. Or would that be a barbershop solo? "Has anybody seen my pal?"

"My pal?"

"My pal?"

"My paaaaalll?" In response to this deep baritone voice, the rubbery ground ripples.

At the crosswalk, a gigantic pink brontosaurus in yellow galoshes looks left and right and left again, afraid to cross. With a deep breath that I can feel ruffle my hair from all the way down here, he takes a single cautious step forward. The ground wobbles. The mice and I pop into the sky with a comic *booiiinnng* sound.

"Watch it, Buster!" the brown mouse cries out, shaking his fist.

The dinosaur steps back, his neck drooping. "Sorry," he apologizes, again frozen at the curb.

"We'll never find her now!" the purple mouse squeaks as they all flop onto their sides. *Find who?* I wonder.

"Where am I?" I ask again.

"No time," the gray mouse says, as all three take a tiny synchronized hop that propels them into the air. This time, they don't land, flying away to who-knows-where to find who-knows-who.

"You new here?" A scraggly girl with a furry face approaches. She has bare feet and a faded floral shawl draped around her shoulders.

I nod. "I guess so."

"Who you looking for?" she asks, as if that's an obvious follow-up question.

I think back to the posters I made right before I found Jack. "I guess me," I state.

She spits on the ground. "That doesn't make any sense."

I shrug. "None of this does. Who are *you* looking for?" I ask in case that's the polite thing to say around here.

"My twin sister. She warned me, but I didn't listen." Her voice cracks.

My heart breaks for this poor bedraggled girl, until I notice something vaguely familiar about her. I squint to picture an oversized hat upon her head. As if by magic, a yellow hat suddenly appears, and before I can even blink, she and I are seated together on a bus that looks like it was yanked out of a cartoon. What the fedora?

My new friend now looks exactly like the mysterious gopher lady. "What's your name?" I ask.

"Miranda," she says, sniffling, equally confused by her new hat and our sudden location change.

"You look just like—"

"George?" a voice interrupts. I glance across the aisle to see what I can only describe as a talking, faceless mop man with at least twenty flopping arms. If he has a face, it's well hidden. The seat beneath him is drenched. "It's been a while!" he exclaims. "What's up, man?" Three of his arms reach across the aisle and wrap around me, pulling me in for a soppy one-sided hug.

"I've seen you before?" I don't understand. I didn't even realize I'd been here before.

"Oh ho, look at you, Mr. High and Mighty," the mop man says. "You don't see me for what, two weeks, and suddenly you've forgotten all about Old Mopsy?"

Two . . . weeks . . . ? What is he talking about?

All of a sudden, the memories come flowing in.

Jack's tenth birthday. Friends over. Real Ones, as his mom so proudly called them.

Me, making an over-the-shoulder wish as Jack blew out his candles that I'd stop being invisible so Jack would stop being embarrassed by me. My spit coating the cake.

Jack, with clenched teeth. "Go away, George." The anger. "Just leave me alone. Go play hide-and-seek or something."

Hiding in the closet. Waiting. Crying. Leaving.

Finding myself here, in this floppy, jiggly nowhere land, with these rejected creatures, all looking for someone and never being found or finding anyone. I was one of them. I am one of them.

"But I went back," I blurt out.

"BACK?!" Miranda and Old Mopsy bellow in unison.

The tires come to a screeching halt. "BACK?!" the bus itself seems to exclaim. Its door swings open, and I assume that's my cue to slip away.

"I should go," I say to my new, or perhaps old, friends just before I race down the aisle and hop off the bus.

So this is what Jack wanted to know. This is where I was, whatever this place is. And I'm like ninety-seven percent sure that his parents aren't here.

I think back to his dad's voicemail that ruined everything, and suddenly I remember what his dad said last: "Friday at one. Our usual barbecue place. Call me back or don't, but I'll be waiting."

That's what Jack needs! I have something actually useful, something that can bring him face to face with his dad, and maybe even his mom, but I'm stuck here. I slowly lift my foot, which feels almost taped to the gooey floor.

How did I get back before? I think of my fliers again. *Have you seen this person?*

I think I went back because Jack was looking for me, though I didn't realize it at the time. There's no hope now. He hates me. He doesn't understand he needs me, but I'm positive he does. "Can you hear me, Jack?" I cry into the Crayola sky. "You may not realize it, but dang it, it doesn't matter because *I* do. You need me, Jack, and somehow, I am going to help you."

An ostrich-like bird that seems too big to be in flight casts a shadow overhead and *caw-caw*s in response. She momentarily blocks out the entire sun, and when the light returns, I find myself back in Jack's house.

I rub the back of my head. "What was that?" I wonder to myself, as I feel the memories of that strange world being plucked from my mind, being replaced with black voids. It's like there are two separate worlds that want nothing to do with each other and the memory of one can't exist in the other. "Miranda?" I whisper before she's gone. "Who's gone?" I ask myself.

I'm shaking, and my head is throbbing, but that doesn't matter. With my legs now intact, I slowly rise to my feet, more determined to help than ever. "Ready or not, Jack, here I come."

CHAPTER 21
JACK

'm somewhere between a "Mom's sick" toss and a "Dad needs to know" turn when a voice *Pssst*s by my side, scaring the heck out of me. The red numbers on Jason's digital clock—*6:18 a.m.*—are the only light in the room, so it takes a moment before I can make out the silhouette of George, kneeling at my bedside.

"We have to go," he whispers.

I throw the covers over my head and groan as though he's woken me up, but honestly, I've been in and out of sleep all night—mostly out, obsessing over my dilemma.

Undeterred, George weasels his head under my covers. In this tight quarter, his breath smells like chocolate-covered strawberries and fish. "I know where your dad is," he says.

"George, please stop."

"I'm serious," he insists, with a gravity in his tone that almost makes me believe him. "I heard the end of the voicemail, and I know where to find him. Your mom might be there, too."

"What?" I cry out, forgetting that sound travels through blankets.

"Jack?" Jason mumbles from his bed.

Crap crap crap, I think to myself, settling deep into the pillow as if this will fool him into thinking I'm sound asleep.

It seems to work. The bed creaks as he adjusts his position, and soon I hear the heavy breaths of my sleeping cousin. "Let's go," I whisper to George.

He bolts out the door. I stop for a moment to rustle through my duffle bag, grabbing my "for emergencies only" phone and my pack of playing cards, the survival gear of champions. After throwing on some shorts, socks, my shoes, and a hoodie I've borrowed from Jason, I'm ready.

Just as I'm about to slip into the hallway, a voice demands from behind, "What are you doing?" I freeze. Jason slides off the bed and hops after me. The air mattress hisses as he steps on top of it. He reaches out to close the door before I can leave, severing my sight of George. I can't lose him again. I don't think you get a fourth chance with this sort of thing.

"I have to go," I plead, knowing all hope is lost.

"It's like six in the morning. Go where?"

A desperate idea springs to my mind. My one chance. I reach out to put my hand on Jason's shoulder. In the dark, I think I end up on his chest, but it'll do. Closer to the heart. "If you had a shot to see your mother one more time before she left, to find out why, to stop her even, would you?"

"Your mom is going to come back, Jack," he promises, sounding so sure it's true.

"In how many 'one more week's?" I push back.

Agonizing silence reigns as Jason mulls my question. Finally, with an intense, clearly conflicted breath, he states, "I will cover for you as long as I can, but you had better be at that table when Dad calls us for lunch. And text me you're alive every hour or all bets are off."

It's easy to agree to this because I'll be reunited with my own parents long before lunch, so it won't even matter. I step forward to hug him, but he's already drifted back into the darkness. "Thank you," I say on repeat. "Thank you. Thank you." Finally,

I pass into the hallway and find George waiting for me, illuminated by a seashell nightlight.

"Follow me," George says. He creeps with his back against the wall, so I do the same. Dark shadows dance against the walls. I should stop this now, but George seems so excited, and he said he'd take me to see my dad. Besides, this is what I've been debating all night anyway. At least George knows where we're going. We tiptoe down the stairs, and George opens the front door.

My stomach feels heavy, momentarily weighing me down and preventing me from taking another step. My eyes dart toward Aunt Rachel and Uncle Dave's closed bedroom door at the top of the stairs. The house is completely silent.

"Ready?" George offers his hand.

With one last quick glance over my shoulder, I take his hand and head into the crisp air outside. It's much lighter already than I expected. The sky is the color of Mom's eyes, and it almost feels like she's watching me, begging me to go back inside. That settles that. Sick or not, I'm still mad at her, so I look up at George and confirm: "Ready."

The soggy grass squishes with each step. My feet sink into the mud, leaving footprints for everyone to follow when they finally get up. Great. At least I have shoes this time.

"Hey. Wait!" There's a tug on my arm. I stop at the edge of the lawn and turn to George. If we're going to do this, we don't have time to wait. I frown, but he can't see it since he's turning to face the house again. "I've got an idea," he says.

Without another word, he starts walking back the way we came. "No. Stop," I beg, looking to my aunt and uncle's window upstairs to make sure their light is still off. It is. "George, get back here!"

He doesn't listen. Before he left, he always used to listen. We always did what I wanted to do, but right now, going back to Aunt Rachel's house is definitely not what I want to do. It took everything inside of me to get this far. George has changed, even during the past week. Do I make everyone sick?

"Jack, get over here!" George calls from the side of the house. I check Aunt Rachel's window once more and slush across the lawn to the garage.

"What are you doing?" I freeze as I watch him push open the side door and walk into the garage. There's a creak from inside the house. I get goosepimply, and my eyes blur as my heart pumps faster. "George, let's just get out of here. They're gonna catch us!"

He ignores me so I follow him inside. Without a light, I can barely make out anything among these metal shelves filled with gardening supplies. Stroking his chin with his fingers, George scans the garage, leaning forward to peer into the particularly dark corners. Leave it to me to have the one imaginary friend in town with a mind of his own. The house creaks again. This time, it's louder and closer. I just know that any minute Aunt Rachel is going to swing open the door and scream—

"AHA!"

My face flushes and I jump about two feet into the air, but it's just George.

"Here we go!" he shouts, waddling over to Morgan's and Jason's bikes, which have been practically in front of him the entire time. The helmets are hanging on the handlebars, and he tosses Jason's helmet to me. Once he has Morgan's helmet on his own head, George taps it with his fist three times. "Perfect," he says, hopping onto her bike. I reluctantly put Jason's helmet on my head. Running away is one thing, but stealing my cousins' bikes?

As if reading my mind, George says, "It's not stealing." He pedals around the garage, getting too close to Aunt Rachel's shiny black car. "It's more like borrowing!" He ends with a squeal and a crash. Now I definitely don't want to be here when Aunt Rachel discovers the brand-new dent on the side of her car, or the side mirror that, in this darkness, I can only imagine is hanging like a drooping flower.

I scramble for Jason's bike, hop on, and pedal as fast as I can. Behind me, I hear a frazzled, slightly stunned George collect Morgan's bike and begin pedaling. We ride down the driveway and along the sidewalk. I can't look at the house, but I'm sure Aunt Rachel's bedroom light is on. She's heard us. I know it. Any minute, Aunt Rachel's car will be right behind us, her half-detached side mirror flapping in the wind. Then we'll really be in for it. What am I doing?

George finally catches up to me, and we ride down the sidewalk, side by side. "Hey, Jack. Slow down!"

I nod but pedal faster. Headlights illuminate the street from behind us. I knew it. The car is going slowly, but the glow of the lights on the street gets brighter and brighter. I grip the handlebars so tightly that I'm sure I'll see handprints when I finally let go.

It's still coming. Closer. Sweat is filling my helmet and dripping down my forehead. Closer. My eyes must be bulging from my head, but I can't see a thing. I don't look back. I can't. Closer.

Closer.

Past.

It's not Aunt Rachel.

The car drives farther away, the taillights getting dimmer and dimmer. I loosen my grip on the handlebars, but only a bit. For the first time since we left, I look over my shoulder. There's nobody there. Aunt Rachel and Uncle Dave still haven't noticed that I'm gone. I picture the empty mattress waiting for me in Jason's room and almost wish I were there now.

George has pulled ahead and begun to whistle. He's taking me to see Dad. Maybe even Mom. And it's what I wanted. I should be thrilled, but all I can think about is Aunt Rachel and Uncle Dave bolting awake after the racket George and I made in the garage. Can I really trust Jason to cover for me? I glance back in their direction one more time.

Where are they?

CHAPTER 22
GEORGE

Riding bikes with Jack is great! At his house, Jack only has one bike so we always had to take turns, and that usually meant Jack took turns around and around and around the street, while I watched. This is a lot more fun.

The city is starting to wake up though, so I should probably decide where we're going to hide until it's time for lunch with his dad.

"Where are we going?" Jack asks from behind me, wondering the same thing I am.

A cluster of trees momentarily blocks out the rising sun. And an idea hits me. *As if by magic.* "Follow me, Jack!" I exclaim, taking a quick left at the corner. He doesn't say anything, but I hear tires spinning on the pavement behind me, so I know he's still following.

In about two minutes, we're at the park. There's nobody here right now, but soon the city will be hopping, and nobody will notice two extra kids in a crowd. It's the perfect place to hang out while I figure out which barbecue place is Jack's parents' "usual."

We drop our bikes near the entrance, and I point to our first stop, far across the green: the tree house. *I told you I'd come back for you*, I mentally comfort the flier that I accidentally littered in the tree more than a week ago.

"My dad's up there?" Jack sounds less confident, but before I can correct him and explain, he's scurrying up the ladder into the tree house. From above, I hear him shout, "Dad!"

Oh dear.

"DAD!" he calls out again, his head emerging through the window of the tree house as he scans the park. It's useless since his dad's not there.

"Mom?" he says, quieter this time. What have I done?

"Jack," I call from below before clutching the first wooden plank on the tree trunk and taking a deep breath. One step at a time, I make my way up the tree with my eyes closed, too scared to look up or down or anywhere at all.

After what feels like forever, my hand reaches up and slaps the floor of the cabin. Thank goodness! I pull myself in. The daylight seems to have filled in since the last time my eyes were open all the way at the bottom of the tree.

The tree house is smaller than I thought it would be, but it's amazing. Four wooden walls, a wooden floor, a slanted wooden roof, three windows, and a door. Scattered leaves and junk decorate the floor. Jack is sitting in the corner, his head resting in his knees, bopping up and down. He's . . . crying?

"Jack?" I approach my best friend cautiously.

His words are so quiet I can barely hear them. "You said he would be here. Why would you lie to me? Again?"

"I didn't say that!" I insist, holding both of my hands out in front of me and glancing at the steep drop behind me. "You misunderstood, Jack!"

He picks up a sheet of loose paper from the floor and crinkles it in his fists. I recognize it immediately as my poster. "Hey, Jack," I exclaim, pointing to the paper. "It's—"

"Blank," he cuts me off, looking first at one side, and then the other. He tosses it aside.

But it's not blank! With a punched-in-the-gut

feeling, I take a step back. The ground beneath my feet is gone! I shriek as I realize I must have just backed out of the tree house door.

My eyes clench closed as my body begins to plummet. "Goodbye, my frie—"

SPLAT. My chest *thunk*s against the wooden floor of the tree house. Huh?

My eyes pop wide open. Jack towers above me as he surges to his feet, but instead of taking my hand to save me from certain death, he points to my legs. When I realize I've only fallen about two feet instead of two hundred, I look down as well. In typical disappearing-act fashion, my legs are gone, jeans and all. My top half is resting on the floor, alone. No wonder I didn't feel the floor beneath me.

I feel incomplete without my legs, and I blush.

"George?" Jack asks, clearly hoping for an explanation as he finally holds out his hand to help.

The moment I take his hand, my legs and pants return, raising me back to Jack's height.

There's no easy way to say it: "I'm disappearing, Jack."

Tears threaten to flow from Jack's eyes again.

"Don't cry. I said I'd take you to your family, and I will. But your dad's message said one o'clock, so I figured we could come here in the meantime."

"It's fine," he says, as though he doesn't even need his parents at this moment. I shouldn't be so selfish, but a smile engulfs my face. It's been so long since he's put me first. "How long have you had the disappearing legs?"

"Since I left you, and it's not always my legs. Arms, ears, spleen, whatever. They come and they go. You get used to it, I guess, but once all of me disappeared and I kind of think it wasn't the first time."

Jack's mouth drops open. "This is all my fault."

I shake my head vigorously. "No, no, no, Jack. Don't say that. It might've even happened before I met you, too. I think that's why I barely remember anything from before then. It's why I'm looking for answers. It's why I need you."

He bites his lip. "George . . ." He sounds like he's about to explain something important, but he doesn't say anything else. I understand. What do you say to somebody who has a bad case of the disappearings?

I don't like how sad he looks, so I change the subject. "Enough about me," I insist. "Let's talk about"—I slyly grin—"oh I don't know. Your favorite barbecue places?"

CHAPTER 23
JACK

Ever since George and I have run away, I can't stop imagining. I don't get it. It's great to have him back, but what I'm imagining now are the real people I know. The ones I left behind. As George goes on listing local barbecue restaurants, I can hardly focus because I keep imagining their faces when they discover I'm gone.

Aunt Rachel's face stretches out really long, her mouth open huge and her eyebrows reaching up to touch the top of her head. Uncle Dave is the opposite. His face squashes together like a squeezed orange with a beard, as he tries to think where I might be.

"Gone?!?!" I imagine Jason saying with a tone of forced surprise as he realizes the jig is up, and we're both busted.

"Dang," Imaginary Morgan says with more curiosity than concern.

I look past George at the brightening sky, the real one outside the real tree house window. It's got to be eight by now. My stomach grumbles. I sure could go for some Crispy Chocolate Bran Flakes with Calcium and Strawberries about now.

". . . Beef Burger Barbecue, not too far from here. And then of course there's that Brazilian BBQ down on Cambridge Street," George rambles on as part of the longest restaurant summary I've ever half-listened to. Apparently he's memorized all the local barbecue restaurants. He must've spent a lot of time on Mom's laptop this week.

This talk of food is not helping anything. With my imaginary cousins haunting my mind and my imaginary friend provoking an empty stomach, I can hardly concentrate, but for whatever reason, this list matters to George, so it matters to me to pretend that it matters to me.

I mindlessly reach for the blank sheet that George insisted was his poster and flip it over. Miraculously, his drawing is now there. *Have you seen this person?* it reads, along with a picture of George. I rub my eyes, not understanding the disappearing and reappearing art. The crudely drawn portrait certainly has a George-ish quality to it, but at the same time, with the gap-teeth and the lost expression, it's remarkably Jack-ish, too. I push down my cowlick as if this drawing is a mirror.

Meanwhile, Imaginary Uncle Dave picks up the phone as Imaginary Aunt Rachel paces the room behind him. "Hello, I'd like to report a missing child," Imaginary Uncle Dave says. I gasp.

"You okay?" George asks, stopping again mid-list.

I assure him I'm fine with a quick smile before Imaginary Morgan runs into my mind and shouts, "And a theft! He stole my bike, Dad! That thief stole my bike, and Jason's too." I like Imaginary Morgan about as much as I like Real Morgan.

"And those are all the barbecue places I know about," George says, finishing with a grand *ta-da* gesture. I clap politely, as if this recitation was a piece of theater.

"Wow," I say, unsure what more he wants from me.

"Any of those sound good?" he prompts when I say nothing else.

My stomach grumbles loudly in response. "It doesn't matter," I tell George. "I don't have any money for food anyway." I study the wooden grain of the floor, running my finger along a jagged crack.

George kneels in front of me. "Okay, Jack, I gotta be real." I frown at the word choice, since he clearly doesn't understand how impossible that is or how it's my fault he's disappearing. He goes on, "Your dad called and told your mom to meet him at their usual barbecue place, but I don't know which that is."

I begin to cackle. Of course there's another obstacle keeping me from my dad. George joins me, throwing his head back and bellowing. Tears begin to stream down my cheeks. I just hope George still thinks I'm laughing. My legs tremble as I rise to my feet. With a lion-esque growl, I rip the flier in two and toss it behind me. "Let's do this," I tell George with a sniffle and a faked confidence. I climb out of the tree house and start down the ladder with absolutely no idea where I'm supposed to go next.

The park is beginning to fill in, and I can hear kids laughing as they run around. When I reach the bottom of the tree, George calls from above: "I'll be down in a minute!" I can practically hear him gulp when he adds, "Or five."

He never was as brave as me. It's how I imagined

him, so I'd never be the most scared person in the room. I'm glad that hasn't changed.

Instead of waiting for George, I trudge across the grass to the bikes. The thing is, in some ways, he *has* changed. I reach out and touch Morgan's bike, running my fingers along the cold metal. Yep. It's really here. I don't understand. Before he left, the stuff George touched only moved in my mind. Nobody saw it. Nobody knew. But there are definitely two bikes here right now.

Is he disappearing or is he turning real?

I reach into my pocket and pull out my "for emergencies only" phone. It's off. As it powers up, Imaginary Aunt Rachel and Imaginary Uncle Dave have just called my Imaginary Parents to tell them they lost their kid. Do my Imaginary Parents even care? Will my real ones?

The phone buzzes in my hands to let me know it's on. I unlock the screen and send Jason a quick text. *I'm alive*, it says.

K, Jason responds almost immediately, as if he's glued to the screen waiting for me. Oddly, it feels kinda nice. I'm glad Dad packed this phone even though he didn't answer when I called. I guess he cares, but he has a funny way of showing it.

Imaginary Dad's not much better. He's a spy. Every time I try to get closer, he slips into the shadows on another secret mission.

And now I have a secret mission, too. I need to find Real Dad, because maybe he doesn't know that Real Mom is sick. Maybe he'll come back to us if he does. Then maybe we'll be happier.

"Where could he be?" Imaginary Aunt Rachel suddenly cries out in my mind, talking about me, not Dad. Uncle Dave puts his arms around her as the imaginary police ring their doorbell.

I think of our door at home. I bet that soon the real police will be breaking it down, looking for us. I know Mom won't like coming home to that kind of mess, but there's nothing I can do now. Real Jack has made a real mess. Tears trickle down Imaginary Aunt Rachel's face, and my own cheeks feel wet, too.

Imaginary Aunt Rachel's sniffling is interrupted by a piggish snort from above. I glance over my shoulder at the tree house. George is almost halfway down, hating every moment. I'm not quite loving this myself, either. Aunt Rachel and Uncle Dave are the only grown-ups who haven't left me, and now I've gone and done something that will freak them out.

My thoughts are interrupted by my phone, which suddenly begins buzzing out of control. I pull it out again. *Missed Call—Mom, Wednesday 9:04 p.m. Missed Call—Mom, Wednesday 12:15 a.m. Missed Call—Mom, Thursday 6:24 a.m.* On and on.

The phone's been off this whole time. Mom has been trying to reach me.

CHAPTER 24
GEORGE

When I finally reach solid ground, my legs collapse beneath me. I grab fistfuls of grass. Land, beautiful land! The visit to the tree house was worth it, though. I've recovered the torn, littered flier, now stuffed in my back pocket, so at least the police won't be after us for littering.

I'm just about to kiss the blessed mud beneath me when a scraggly voice calls out, "Hey you!" I almost glance in her direction, but there are a few more people at the park now, so I'm sure she's not talking to me.

"Walrus!" she continues. Then again . . .

My head whips to the right. "Yes?"

My mouth nearly drops to the ground when I see the speaker: the gopher lady from the bus ride to the zoo. I can't even believe it. I push myself up to my feet.

The gopher lady looks cautiously over her shoulder before joining me under the tree house. I follow the gaze of her plum-colored eyes. Her friend, the little boy from the bus, is having an early morning brunch-nic with his mom.

"What do you think you're doing?" she demands, turning her attention back to me. Her breath smells like coffee.

"I'm sorry," I tell her. "I can't talk now. I've got to get to Jack." I glance toward my best friend. He's obsessing about something on his phone and not paying any attention to me at all.

"Is that your friend from before?"

"Yes! Isn't it great?"

Her gopher-face scrunches up. "You've got to stop chasing him," she says solemnly. "Find a new friend, someone who believes, or disappear for good."

How does she know what I do and don't need to do? Just because she sees me and talks to me doesn't mean she knows me at all.

My heart is urging me to turn around and tell Jack it's time to go, but my feet won't listen. "Jack and I are best friends," I insist, "And he needs me."

"For how long?" she asks, again looking over at her boy, who pops a tiny blueberry muffin into his mouth. Silence follows as I remember Jack not wanting me before and the giant fight we had yesterday. This seems to be all the answer she needs. "Do what you have to do, but don't say I didn't warn you." She reaches out and pats my arm. "Take care." With that, she turns her back on me and begins to walk toward her friend.

A name flashes to my mind out of nowhere, and I call out after her, "Miranda!"

She whips around so quickly that her hat flies off her head. "What did you call me?" She strides back up to me and slams me against the tree. "Where did you hear that name?" Well, this has taken a turn!

"I—I can't remember."

"Try," she says, pushing me harder. The rough bark scrapes at my back through my T-shirt. I'd normally be terrified, but she doesn't seem angry, just desperate, maybe even afraid.

I close my eyes and try to remember. My knees wobble. Or is that the ground? In the darkness of my mind, I see a rainbow. And a mop. He's talking. And this gopher lady in a tattered cloak. My eyes open, taking in the similar features of the gopher lady in front of me. Her nose twitches. "She's looking for you," I say.

She steps back, her grip loosened, but still not letting go.

"I'm sorry," I say. "That's all I remember."

"Hey, you!" Jack calls out, noticing us for the first time. "Get your hands off of him."

The gopher lady releases me, and we both stare as Jack rushes up to us. He puffs out his chest to seem extra scary but deflates it once he observes my chuckle.

"You are not gonna believe this, Jack," I begin, not even sure how to explain the situation or who this creature is.

Jack stares at her with his mouth open. "You're right," he agrees.

"You can see me?" she asks. He nods. That seems to mean something different to each of them. The gopher lady tips her head, seemingly impressed, while Jack's eyes read more puzzled. "Then tell your friend he's a chicken-headed noodle-brain."

Jack snorts.

"Excuse me?" I demand.

"You saw my sister. You know your fate."

She scans Jack from his sneakers to his bed head.

Her next warning is to him. Wagging a furry finger in his face, she says, "He needs to move on soon, and so do you. I saw him flickering. If you don't let him go, you know what will happen."

She has such a commanding way with words that all a stunned Jack can do is nod again. His stomach grumbles, filling the silence that follows. The gopher lady turns to her friend at the picnic bench. When he looks up, she pantomimes eating a fruit, then tilts her head to Jack. The boy says something to his mother, who seems to agree, before he fills a tiny plate with food and joins us under the tree.

"Hungry?" he asks Jack, offering the entire plate.

Jack greedily grabs it, stuffing his mouth with a piece of melon before recalling his manners. "Fank you," he says as he chews. "Fank you show much."

"Your folks forget to feed you?" the gopher lady asks Jack, as both she and the boy stare at Jack slurping up food with a hint of disgust in their eyes.

"His parents are gone," I explain, only to throw my hands over my mouth, realizing I've said too much. Sure, they brought us food, but they're stranger-ish, and we're on the run. We shouldn't be trusting anyone. "I mean, we're staying with his aunt and uncle. We got up at five to do some working out so we're hungry again." I bench-press the air to demonstrate, then grimace and stop partway because it's heavier than I thought.

The gopher lady's boy snorts.

"Wait. *You* can see me?" I ask.

He nods.

My face lights up.

The gopher lady puffs up and wedges herself between us. "He's mine," she warns.

Before I can respond, Jack's pants begin buzzing. He drops the plate and reaches into his pocket, spilling the remaining pieces of fruit.

"Jack! We just picked up the last bit of litter!" I scold him, bending down to gather up his mess.

"It's her!" he cries out.

I snap back to attention. "Rachel?" My heart races, as my body prepares to flee in case we're busted and need to get outta here fast.

"Rachel?" the gopher lady repeats softly, as if she recognizes the name.

"No." Jack shushes us with a swish of his hand. He taps *answer* and brings the phone to his ear. Breathlessly, he says: "Mom?"

CHAPTER 25
JACK

"You're not going to believe what's happened, Jacky!" Mom exclaims, jumping right in without even a *Hello* or an *I missed you.* "Go on. Guess!"

"Ummmmm." I scan through the possibilities. You've reconnected with your ex-imaginary friend, found out your mother is sick, learned that your absent father may in fact want to be with you, and run away from your temporary home to find him at a mystery barbecue restaurant? That doesn't seem right. "I don't know."

"Oh, you're no fun," she jokes. It stings a little.

My arms shake, and my pits drip as I wait for the big reveal. "Come on. Tell me," I plead, trying to match her enthusiasm but dreading another bombshell.

"Okay fine, fine, fine," Mom agrees, before singing, "I've fallen in loooooove!"

"What?!"

George flinches with surprise when I shout. The furry lady and the freckled fruit kid stare at me, too, anxiously waiting as if they understand the half of it. I hear Morgan's mocking swoon replay in my mind, and now I know exactly why Jason deleted that voicemail at Aunt Rachel's house. Mom's found someone special, too. "Mom, are you serious?"

Mom laughs gleefully. "I'm excited, too, sweetie. And it's all because of you." Well, I'm glad someone's finally said it. "I told you I'd make you proud."

"Mom, how does falling in love—"

She doesn't let me finish. "I knew you wanted nothing more than to find your friend, so when I got out at the rest stop off 95 to pee, I went around calling his name, until this dream man, MY Greg, heard me and responded. He rides a bike." She giggles.

"It's George," I correct her for the five-hundredth time.

"Oh my God," Mom says. "Hon. Hon," she calls to somebody on her end of the line. "The wombat's name is George." A man snorts. Mom laughs so hard she begins wheezing. I pull the phone a few inches away from my face and wait for her to finish sharing a laugh with some biker named Greg. I can almost picture him now. Silver hair that swishes in the breeze when he removes his helmet. A heart tattoo with the name of someone else's mom he's previously stolen peeking out beneath a tattered black sleeve.

"What's the joke?" George asks, able to hear Mom's ecstasy.

I frown. "I am."

George bristles at this and reaches out to steal the phone from me. "Why I oughtta—!"

"*Stop!*" I shout, pushing him back.

"Stop what?" Mom says, returning to our conversation.

"Nothing," I say.

"I've missed you, Jacky," she says, still recovering her breath. I feel like a chump when my insides flutter. It's the first kind thing she's said to me so far, and I totally eat it up. "What've you been up to?" she asks.

My mind races through everything that's happened. Everything she's missed. Everything I've learned. I'd get in so much trouble for ninety percent of it, and who knows how she'd respond to the rest. "Nothing," I say again instead, before deciding to press my luck. "Are you okay, Mom? Aunt Rachel says you're sick."

"She said *what*?" There's a shocked silence. "Who does she think she is, turning you against me like that?" Her tone instantly softens. "Oh, sweetie. I can't believe she would say that to you. You don't need to worry. I'm fine. I'm great." After a pause, she adds. "If I were sick, could I do this?" I wonder what in the world she's doing on the other end of the phone as she cries out, "Woohoohoohoo!" Standing on her head? Juggling flaming batons? Whatever it is, it sounds like a healthy woohoo.

Maybe she's right, but why would Aunt Rachel lie? To keep me from running away? I look around the park. That went well. I change the subject: "Are you coming home soon?"

There's an uncomfortable silence as Mom mulls the question around in her mind. The pause is all I need to confirm I've made the right decision. Sick or not, Mom doesn't want me. I need to find Dad.

"I have a question," I say, saving her from the struggle of finding a polite way to say *I'm all set never seeing you again.*

"What's that?" she asks.

I have to do this carefully. "So. I was talking to, uh, Morgan," I begin. "And she wanted to know if there were any, um, barbecue restaurants, that you could recommend."

George catches on to my scheme and gives me a grinning thumbs-up.

"What kind of barbecue?" Mom asks with a hint of suspicion.

I bite my lip as I try to figure out the best way to get the answer I need. "A sentimental one. Any you used to go to with, um, oh, I don't know . . ." I nearly whisper as I finish, "Dad?"

Any sort of bouncing-on-the-couch-in-love sweetness is gone when Mom replies, "I swear to God. Did your father call you?"

"No. He doesn't have my number," I say, which is true.

"Oh my God, Jack. He's turning you against me, too. Just like Rachel. That son of a—"

"MOM," I snap back. "Tell me the damn barbecue!" George, furry-face, and freckle-fruit all gasp. I've never spoken to anyone like that, especially my mom.

"I want to speak to Rachel," she insists.

"She's at work," I spit back, which is probably true by now.

"Dave, then," she commands.

"He's . . . busy right now." Mom's clearly onto me and is about to ask for Jason or Morgan. "I have to go play cards with Jason," I say, ending this before it gets ugly.

"Jack, if I find out you've gone to Daddy-O's, I'll . . ." She trails off. I think I hear a sob. "I have to call your father." With a click, the line goes dead.

"Mom?" I say to the empty phone. A series of beeps confirms that once again, she's gone. I drop my arm.

George looks at me expectantly. "So how's yer mommmmm?"

"In love," I respond. "And about to ruin everything."

CHAPTER 26
GEORGE

Jack takes my hand. "We have to go."

The gopher lady steps in front of us. "To your aunt Rachel's," she commands.

"Who *are* you?" Jack asks, which is so rude since they were just talking like five minutes ago. He starts to go around her. The gopher lady closes her eyes, inhales deeply, and clenches her jaw before exhaling into her cheeks. She expands like a self-inflating balloon, becoming larger and blocking our path.

Jack and I stumble backward.

With another quick gasp, she sucks in more air and again increases in size on the exhale. She's a foot taller than us now.

"She's biggifying herself!" I cry out in horror.

"Listen to me," she says, her voice so much deeper

that the ground seems to tremble. She lunges forward, arms outstretched to grab me. I hadn't noticed those claws before!

I try to run but my feet are glued to the grass as if by magic. "Holy mole lady!" I shriek.

Jack's feet are fortunately not stuck, and with a quick tug, he pulls me aside in the nick of time. Her arms envelop the empty air, and she ends in a self-embrace as Jack and I dash across the park. We snatch our bikes and ride into the city beyond.

"Find Rachel!" the gopher-werewolf-balloon-lady-monster howls from beneath the tree house, but at least she doesn't chase us.

After a thirty-minute ride, we find ourselves at the Bath Stuff and Such where I wrote Jack his letter. "In here," I say to Jack, taking the lead, glad that he can finally read about everything he missed. We dump our bikes by the entrance. After two spins through the revolving doors, the warm sixties pop music reassures us that we are finally safe. The cashier is busy scratching the scruffy hairs on his chinny chin chin. "I'm back," I announce to nobody.

"You've been here before?" Jack asks, wiping sweat from his forehead and scanning the giant store, one magnificent display at a time.

"And I have something for you!" The next few minutes are a blur as I race around the store, towing Jack behind. I point out all the key landmarks. "That's where I borrowed some paper," and "That's where I met Stanley the alien," and "That's where I wanted to take a bath before I disappeared all the way to your house."

I race down the aisle, towing Jack behind. Jack's steps are not as quick as mine. My arm almost feels as if it'll pull from its socket with his weight, but I'm sure he's just going slowly to take it all in. He pants, "Slowdowgeorge," hardly able to get the words out.

"What?" I ask, glancing behind me.

"Slow down this instant," snaps a voice in front of me that isn't mine or Jack's. I look to see who's there, but it's too late because I've just crashed into her. "What the hedgehog," shrieks the woman that I've crashed into, but with a ruder word. "What are you doing?"

"Sorry." Jack's breathing so hard he can hardly answer her. "We were . . . We were . . . We were . . ." He takes a deep breath and tries again: "Running, ma'am. We were running."

His panicked eyes shift to me as I scoot right next to the lady. With my hands on my hips and my mouth in a serious straight line, I mimic the woman to extract a laugh out of poor frightened Jack. "Weeeeeeeee?" she asks. "Who is this weeeeeeeeeee, young man?" She points to him. "I just see youuuuuuuuuu." Finally a perk of being invisible.

"Fine. *Iiiiiiiiiiiiiii* was running," he says, before joining me in uncontrollable laughter.

That's when the lady says, "Well! *Iiiiiiiii* would like to speak with one of your parents."

Between fits of laughter, Jack gasps, "Me too." Breaking into a fit of giggles, Jack and I skirt around her and walk away.

"Do you want to try out my canopy bed?" I ask. "I left the letter I wrote you under my pillow. Now you can read it!"

Before Jack can answer, a voice says, "Annnnd sent." We turn to find a kid with hair that sticks up in all the right places wearing a crimson collared shirt with a tiny alligator (or is it a crocodile?). He sits on the model bed that used to be mine, looking like he just won the lottery, tapping away on the fanciest-looking phone I've ever seen.

"George," Jack says to the stranger. This kid stole my name!

"Morgan said we had to lay off," Not-Me-George

says with a smirk. "Be nice. That it was just your mom, and you were okay. This'll show her."

"Huh?" Jack and I say in unison. "Show her what?"

"That you're just like your mom. A lunatic running around in a store, making a scene, and embarrassing everyone."

"Don't you dare say that about my mother!" Jack lunges forward as Not-Me-George snaps up a pillow to protect himself, revealing my letter. I grab the back of Jack's shirt, trying to hold him back, but my arms still feel like absolute noodles after benchpressing the air earlier. I'm useless.

"What the fluff, man?" Not-Me-George says, using an actual curse, crouching farther up the bed. My letter crinkles beneath his feet. He throws the pillow at Jack. It whacks him in the head, which seems to snap him out of his rage.

Jack bats the pillow onto the ground and looks at me. "Morgan knows where we are now. We have to get out of here." We turn our backs on the other George only to find the furious lady we crashed into standing next to an official Bath Stuff and Such security guard.

"HERE HE IS!" she cries out. Not-Me-George snickers, pulling out his phone for another video.

I'm in panic mode, but Jack plays it as cool as possible, saying in his sweetest voice, "Is there a problem, Officer Stuff and Such, sir?"

"Where're yer parents, kid?" he asks.

"Wish I knew," Jack replies.

One of the officer's eyebrows goes up while the other one goes down.

"No respect," *tsks* the lady.

"All right, ma'am. I'll take it from here." He shoos her away with a swish of his hand. I do the same with both hands for dramatic effect. "Follow me, kid," he tells Jack.

"And they never saw him again," Not-Me-George chuckles maniacally, adding a chillingly effective bit of drama to his little phone video.

The officer shoots him a look. "You a part of this?"

Not-Me-George turns a shade of red that almost matches his shirt, shaking his head frantically. "Sir. No, sir! Sorry, sir." His arms drop and without another word, he's running away to the bath section of the store. Coward.

Officer Stuff and Such rolls his eyes. "Punk." Except for the fact that he's about to arrest us, I like this guy. Returning his attention to Jack, he says, "Come on."

"Wait," Jack says. He points to a woman all the way in the kitchen department. "That's my mom," he lies, waving to her and smiling his cutest smile. She isn't paying attention, but if she were, she would not have waved back or smiled, because she is certainly not Jack's mom.

"Follow me," the officer says, marching toward the poor lady who is about to be scolded to keep a better eye on the bothersome son that she didn't even know she had. As soon as the officer's back is to us, I'm pulling Jack's arm in the other direction.

When the officer reaches the lady, she growls and calls out an angry "GEEEEEORGE," but I know I'm not the George she's looking for.

"And they never saw him again," I whisper to Jack, who chuckles at this good fortune of accidentally busting an enemy.

No time to celebrate, as Officer Stuff and Such has noticed we're gone, and his eyes are scanning the store. He'll never see us again though, because we are sneaking, and we are hiding, and we are dashing, and we are darting, and we are running out the door, and we are sprinting down the sidewalk, and we are safe, and we are laughing and laughing and laughing.

CHAPTER 27
JACK

When we've stopped laughing and I've caught my breath, I shake the silliness from my head. "We have to find my dad," I insist, a sense of urgency returning to my voice.

"What do you think we're doing?" George asks, scratching his head. "Once we find the barbecue—"

"No," I interrupt. "We need to find him now. Mom's probably already called him and told him not to meet us, and you know Morgan'll sic her parents on us the second she sees that video. We're wasting time!"

George throws his hands in the air dramatically. "Well, what are we supposed to do? Your dad didn't exactly give us his address."

He's right. Except . . . I look more closely at George. "Did he ever tell you?"

George seems stunned by the question. "When he packed your stuff?"

I shake my head. "When you went out for coffee."

"When we went where for what?" He sticks out his tongue. "Blech."

"Now bear with me," I say.

"Bear?!" George freaks out, clutching my arm and frantically looking from one side of the street to the other. "Did that gopher-monster follow us?"

I slide my arm out from his grasp. "No. Listen. The last time I talked to my dad, he said he loved your jokes. He said he had coffee with you once a week."

George furrows his brow. "I think I'd remember that." He frowns and murmurs, "Wouldn't I?" He rubs his temples and shakes his head around a bit, as if checking whether the memory is in there. "Those hilarious jokes do sound like me."

I know it never happened, but he's imaginary, right? I've . . . enhanced his memories before. Heck, even *he* has, with his walrus family and the card tricks. "I . . . seem to recall you mentioning it," I say.

George's eyes bulge in disbelief, really bringing out his walrus side.

I continue. "It was right around the corner from

here. The Starbucks with the outdoor patio." I take his hand and together we head in that direction. "The green and white umbrellas were open, blocking out that blazing summer sun. Dad was wearing his gray suit, without a tie. He was on his lunch break, and he wanted to be casual."

"For his friend," George finishes my sentence uncertainly, a glimmer of a memory forming. "For me." There's a glaze in his eyes.

I go on. "He ordered—"

"A hot chocolate," George finishes my sentence, hypnotically. "One for each of us. Extra whipped cream and chocolate sprinkles on mine."

"That's right," I said. "You were slaying him with your best jokes."

"Like the one about the oak tree and the bluebird in roller skates."

"Yes," I confirm, wishing I could hear the joke myself, but afraid to stray from the task at hand. "'What's new?' my dad said next."

"Not much, Jack's dad. Where do you live now?"

George is playing along beautifully. It's working. "And what did he say?"

He recites: "'Across town.' Then I shared the joke about the no-eye deers."

Across town? That can't be right. How could he be so close all this time and never come to visit? There must be a mistake. "Enough with the jokes, George," I insist.

"Your dad seemed to like 'em. We don't have much else in common." He shakes his head. "Anyway, he said he had to go. He finished his drink really quickly."

"But first," I say, "he ordered a ride home and you read his address on his phone, over his shoulder."

"No," George pushes back.

This isn't how imagining works. He's supposed to be doing what I want him to be doing, but he's making it all wonky.

"He told me the joke about the baby ostrich disguised as a glove, and he passed on his best to my uncle Chester." George does a double-take. "Wait. So Chester is real?" He's beginning to come out of this haze.

"Yes," I say, going along with this because it's my only hope. "And I seem to recall you telling me that next, my dad said he wanted to exchange Christmas cards with Chester, so he gave you a tiny slip of paper with his address."

"Oh yeah," George recalls, nodding. "He slid me a business card."

"And what did that say?" I ask, desperately.

George shrugs and maintains a steady tone. "I didn't read it."

"OH, COME ON!" I shout at George, nearly pulling him from this trance completely.

"It was for Chester." Realization dawns in George's increasingly alert eyes. He's devastated when he says, "I forgot to pass along your dad's regards." He kicks the concrete.

We've arrived at the Starbucks with the umbrellas wide open. George takes in the scene and nods. "I remember it as if it were today," he says dreamily. "After a few more jokes, he said he really had to go. Your dad asked me to take care of you. Can you imagine? Me taking care of you?"

Maybe not, but my dad's concern still feels kinda nice, even if I can only feel it through George's pretend memory.

"As he waited for his ride, he started talking about this woman—"

"That's enough," I say, before the *someone special* can destroy my positive mood. "You know," I say, looking at George thoughtfully, "my mom might also know my dad's address."

George scrunches up his nose. "You think

she'd give it to you though, after what you just said to her?"

"No." I look my best friend in the eye. "But I was just remembering the time you teleported to meet Mom and her new boyfriend and asked her for Dad's address."

George's eyes widen. "When was that?"

I'm sorry, George, I think to myself, as I say, "Now."

He holds his hands up in front of him protectively and takes a cautious step back. "No, no, no, no . . ." he mutters.

He disappears before my eyes. As if by magic.

CHAPTER 28
GEORGE

A cart filled with black suitcases whizzes across the speckled tile floor, as a fuzzy intercom voice mumbles, "Final boarding call for Flight 1042 to Cincinnati." Colorful travel posters decorate the walls, like the ones in Jack's cousin's room.

"What am I doing at an airport?" I mutter to myself. I don't even know what city I'm in. The way Jack just swooshed me away like that is, well, unbelievable. I know I teleported on my own once, but this is different. He's never done that to me before. I frown, wondering how he did it—and wondering how the helicopter I'm supposed to get back home again.

I scan the airport and discover Jack's mom walk-ing toward the security line, wearing ripped blue jeans and a black T-shirt. Her hair is dirtier and shorter than I remember. Some guy desperately clutches her hand like he's afraid she'll slip away. "Who's that?" I ask out loud.

"Who's what? What do you see?" Jack's voice sounds in my ear.

"What the hexagon!" I shout at the unexpected exclamation. I jump about a hundred feet into the air and whip my head from side to side.

Jack is nowhere to be seen, but he comes in loud and clear as he snaps, "George! Where's my mom?"

Well, this is a new one. I realize I must be wearing a headset, and when I reach up, sure enough, I find a small gadget hooked around my ear.

"Where did this headset come from?" I ask, wondering if Jack was wrong about me not being magic, just like he was wrong about my uncle not being real.

Ignoring my question, he says, "What's she doing?"

I glance back in his mom's direction. "Getting on a plane, maybe? Lemme check." I creep closer.

She slaps her ticket and her license on the ticket checker's desk. A security guard stands not too far away, arms crossed, eyes on them. The checker and the guard both have glistening golden badges, popping against their royal-blue button-downs and fancy black neckties. I describe the scene for Jack.

"Ticket to where?" he demands.

I try to get closer, but his mom's friend is blocking my view. Since I am still one hundred percent invisible, no "Excuse me" will help.

"Her friend is in the way," I regretfully explain.

"Friend?" Through gritted teeth, Jack snarls, "Describe him."

I study the stranger. His tattoos. His baggy clothes. His salt-and-pepper hair. "He won't let go of your mom's wrist," I say to Jack, going back to that one tiny detail and ignoring everything else. I'm no expert at hand holding, but I think it's usually mutual. There's something almost vise-like about his grip.

With her free hand, Jack's mom struggles to stuff her license into a tiny purse. No wonder she left her pills at home. There's barely any room for anything in this bag.

"I have to go," Jack's mom tells her friend, tipping her head toward the nearly empty security line just on the other side of the counter. The stranger doesn't set her free.

"Sir," the ticket checker warns him. "Ticketed passengers only."

Jack's mom spins around to face the stranger. He finally releases her hand, which she wraps around his neck. And they kiss. Like a lot. Right in front of the airport security staff. Travelers stop to stare. A man with white hair peeking out of his ears grumbles "Outta my way" as he bumps them aside to have his own ticket checked. The kissing continues.

"Oh my God," I say in disbelief.

"What's happening?" Jack cries out, terrified, followed by "Ask her about my dad." I'm pretty sure she doesn't want to think about Jack's dad right now, and I don't want to get any closer to this.

Apparently, the security guard does. "Miss," she warns Jack's mom, as if it's all her fault. Finally, the smooch comes to an end.

Jack's mom has tears in her eyes as she steps away. "I have to go."

Her friend suddenly looks furious as he snatches her wrist back. "Don't leave."

"I'll be back," she promises. She draws a little cross over her heart with her free hand.

"Liar," he barks.

"Let me go," she commands, but he doesn't. Well, that does it. Jack's mom has never been my favorite human in the world, but nobody holds her like that and gets away with it. I stride up to the pair.

"Get your hands off of her," the security guard and I both say at the same time. The officer seems a little hesitant to get more involved than that, keeping a safe distance. *Coward*, I think, charging at the man and kicking him in the shin. He releases Jack's mom at once.

"What the hemisphere was that?" he says, using a nastier word, and looking down in my direction but seeing nothing.

He could feel that?

The stranger's fiery eyes shoot up to the guard, as if it was her. Yet another perk of being invisible.

Jack's mom takes advantage of the distraction to race to the security line. She throws her shoes and purse into a banged-up plastic bin, then looks over her shoulder, shaking, with tears flowing down her cheeks. With both the security guard and me prepared to intervene again if necessary, the strange man doesn't follow. Instead he curses at her: "They'll just reject you again, you stupid—" I kick him again before he can finish the sentence. "SON OF A . . ." He bends down to rub his leg.

"What is going on?" Jack demands in my ear. "Where's my mom?"

Oh no.

She shuffles through the metal detector in bare feet.

I race after her.

BEEP BEEP BEEP BEEP BEEP BEEP BEEP! the metal detector screams as I shoot through, red lights flashing. A security guard looks in my direction like he's seen a ghost. I lift my hand and pat the small contraption hooked around my ear that caused this racket.

On the other side of the security checkpoint, I look around but don't see Jack's mom. I was too slow. I've ruined everything. I can barely hear myself as I whisper to Jack with a quiver in my voice, "She's gone."

With that, the airport fades from view, turning to black. In a moment, my eyes are overwhelmed by the glowing sun. The shapes of the outdoor Starbucks seating return, Jack by my side. He doesn't have to say anything. I can read the devastation in his eyes. I've failed him again. "I'm sorry," I tell my best friend.

His sadness only lasts a moment before his eyes light up. "Remember that time you went through Aunt Rachel's address book?"

No. No, I do not remember that! I begin to disappear.

"No, wait!" Jack says, "Even better, when you were actually at my dad's house!" I feel a tear in my chest as if Jack's thoughts are about to rip me in two and send me hurtling in different directions, chasing after more memories that I'm pretty sure are not real. I cry out in pain, clutching my chest and leaning forward to squish my belly back together.

"STOP!" I cry out. "STOP IT! STOP IT!"

With a gasp, Jack's eyes widen. He looks as though I've smacked him in the face.

My whiskers bristle as my nostrils flare. *"Stop trying to change me!"*

A blankness settles over Jack's entire face, and I realize I've just swooshed his mind away to who-knows-where, just like he did to me. I wave my hand in front of his eyes. "Jack? Jack? You okay, Jack?" I ask with a hint of panic in my voice. But it's useless. He's gone.

CHAPTER 29
JACK

As George cries out "Stop trying to change me," I'm taken back to a time shortly before my dad left. The words, those exact words, are what my mom begged of my dad right before the bowl of pancake batter dropped from her arms and clattered onto the floor.

It was at that very moment that I entered the kitchen. "What was that?" I asked innocently. Neither of my parents responded, instead both watching the lumpy sand-colored batter ooze across the yellowing linoleum.

"Look what you've done," my dad finally said, rising from the table to grab a towel and mop up the mess.

"I'm sorry," Mom and I both muttered, me out

of habit, but I'm pretty sure this was not my fault.

"You're not trying," Dad said, again to Mom.

Her arms went limp. The metal whisk slipped from her hand, too, landing in the inedible mush with a tiny splash and vibrating *boiiiiiing* sound. "And you have all the answers?"

I didn't know what they were talking about. All I knew was that I wasn't having pancakes for breakfast. Unsure what more to say or do, I squeezed past Mom to grab my Crispy Chocolate Bran Flakes with Calcium and Strawberries from the pantry.

"Jack, will you get out of here?" Dad commanded.

"But the pancakes—" I began to explain, pointing to the mess as if it wasn't what we were all thinking about anyway.

"Now!"

I looked to my mom, who pouted her lips but nodded in agreement. She raised her fingers to the side of her head and gently massaged her temples. It's her disappointed pose, but for once, her eyes turned from me to my dad, on his hands and knees sopping up our overturned breakfast.

"We'll talk later, Jack," she promised softly with a quiver in her voice.

I exited the kitchen into the living room. "What

was that about?" I asked out loud as I approached the sofa. Nobody answered, which made sense, since there was nobody there. I scanned the room and realized for the first time that I hadn't seen George in months.

◆

George is waving his hands in front of my face, up and down, up and down, as my mind ventures back to the real world. What was my dad trying to change? Why did my mom look so scared? So helpless? And how delicious do pancakes sound right now?

My stomach growls, bringing George and the coffee shop fully back into focus. He recognizes the change, that I'm back, and he grins for a moment, before averting his eyes and harrumphing, still hurt by me taking advantage of him like that.

"I'm sorry," I say, imagining somebody sticking their grubby hands into my mind and changing everything I know about myself. I can't help but wonder if that's how Mom feels as we each try to force her back into our own versions of normal. Aunt Rachel. Dad. Me. I stretch my arm out and pat George's shoulder. "I won't do it again," I promise.

He smiles, although I can tell he's not quite convinced. "I'm so confused," he finally says.

"Me, too," I have to admit.

"Why's it always me, Jack?" he asks. "Why can I be swooshed away to nowhere? Why am I disappearing? Why do I always have to be the invisible one?"

I bite my lip and scan the parking lot. Mom swooshed me away to Rachel's after Dad acted like I was invisible, so I made myself disappear, and nobody noticed. George is less alone than he thinks. Still, I've only disappeared temporarily, and George . . . I look at his expectant eyes, waiting for me to make things better.

The gopher lady told me I had to let him go, to set him free, or he'd disappear forever, and here I am selfishly gripping him tighter and tighter when I know as soon as I find one of my parents . . . A lump forms in my chest as I realize what I need to do next.

I try to blink back my tears to hide them from George, but it's too late. Concern spreads over his face, as a smile stretches across mine. I have an idea. A final adventure, a way to give him exactly what he wants: to be seen. I break the silence with a snort to sniff up my snot and say to George, "Maybe you don't have to be."

My answer takes George by complete surprise. He does a dramatic double take. "I beg your pardon?"

"Maybe you don't always have to be the invisible one." That sparks a tiny, hopeful twinkle in his eye. "I have an idea," I say, taking his hand and leading him down the sidewalk. "Do you trust me?"

He nods. Before I know it, we're right beside the fountain where George and I once watched the world's most horrible magician. He kept trying all these stupid card tricks on us but never seemed to guess our card right. He ended up spilling his cards all over the sidewalk, but George and I clapped anyway because we didn't want to be rude. "Do you know where we are?" I ask George.

He shrugs. "Haymarket?"

"Ho ho no," I laugh. Noting the large sign labeling the Haymarket train station next to me, I add, "Well. Yes. But it's so much more than that, George." Inching closer to the fountain, I say, "This is a magical place where dreams come true."

George crosses his arms.

"Don't believe me?" I point to the water. "Just look." George and I peer down. The bottom of the fountain is covered with tiny silver and copper circles. "People throw money here all the time to earn the favor of the fountain's magical forces."

George scrunches up his eyebrows. "You mean we're gonna steal the money?"

I can feel my face flush. As if we need to add more thievery to our list of offenses. "No," I quickly correct him. "We're gonna make magic."

"We're gonna do what?"

"You said you wanted me to see your tricks," I say. "But how would you like other people to see them, too?"

All traces of George's sadness are gone. "But nobody ever sees me!"

"Until now," I say. "Don't you think it's time that the world meets . . ." I pause to think. Waving my arms dramatically, I announce, "The Great Georgini!"

A contagious grin spreads across George's face before finding its way to mine.

CHAPTER 30
GEORGE

This. Is. Amazing.

Jack pulls the pack of cards from his pocket. "I just need you to tell me how your tricks work."

"Jack. Jack, Jack, Jack, Jack, Jack," I scold, wagging my finger at him. "A magician never reveals his secrets."

Mischief creeps into his eyes as he counters, "Sharing secrets is what friends are for."

I squint, trying to sort this one out. He's got me there. "I guess you're right."

"Great!" he exclaims. "Now if you can just lead me through your tricks step by step, then all these folks"—he gestures toward the people walking by—"will see your magic and know just how amazing the Great Georgini can be!"

At this point, my smile is practically wrapped around my head.

"Whenever you're ready," Jack says, "just tell me what to do."

"Excuse me, everyone. May I have your attention please," I say. Jack doesn't move. I wave my arms in a frantic circle, encouraging him to repeat the words. "Come on," I whisper. "Say it!" A man on his phone rushes past.

"Excuse me, everyone," Jack mumbles.

"LOUDER!" I insist.

He sighs, before shouting out, "MAY I HAVE YOUR ATTENTION PLEASE!"

Yes! I think, but I don't say that out loud because I don't want Jack repeating it. Instead I say, "Presenting the magic act of the Great Jackaroni."

Jack pauses. *What?* his eyes ask, before his mouth reluctantly echoes my words. My heart skitters in anticipation. A nice lady and her daughters stop.

"Look," a boy says, taking his grandmother's hand and directing her to Jack. No: to the Great Jackaroni!

I walk over to the boy. "Choose him," I tell Jack.

"Choose . . ." Jack freezes, realizing that's an action command, not a speaking one. "You there," he says, pointing to the same boy. Very smooth, buddy. I wink at my best friend. "Will you please pick a card, any card?" Jack and I say at the same time. He's getting it! I must be a really good teacher.

The boy releases his grandmother's hand and hurries over to Jack. Two men in business suits pause to observe the scene. The boy snatches a card. Another woman with two shopping bags also comes to a stop.

"Please, don't show me the card, but let the audience see," I instruct. Jack repeats my words as a few more people stop to stare. Our audience. They're watching my magic. They're watching me.

"Is your card . . ." the Six of Hearts flashes before my eyes. "The Six of Hearts?"

When Jack exclaims, "The Six of Hearts," the crowd breaks into gentle applause.

"Lucky guess," one girl shouts. "I didn't even see you shuffle. This thing is rigged."

Jack's face flushes. I guess one problem with being famous like us is that not everybody will be so quick to believe, but it's okay. "Hand her the deck," I tell Jack. "Tell her to shuffle."

Jack does, and the girl agrees. At my and Jack's commands, she takes a card, any card, shows the audience, reshuffles it into the deck, and hands the deck to Jack.

"Now," I say to Jack, "throw the cards into the air."

"And now," Jack says, "I will . . ." He pauses, suddenly processing the genius behind this trick, no doubt. "Throw the cards into the air?" he adds.

Every eye is fixed on him. I scoot closer to his side so that some of them will also be fixed on me during our finest moment. "Trust me, Jack."

He closes his eyes before hurling the cards above his head. "Yes!" I shout, watching some get caught in the wind and others fall into the fountain behind. "Yes, yes, yes!" I'm laughing so hard that the Great Jackaroni cannot help but open his eyes and smile.

As the last cards settle to the ground, a hush falls over the crowd.

Jack and I turn our attention to the sidewalk, where most of the cards rest, all facedown except for one. The Nine of Clubs.

The silence is pierced by the girl's voice: "That's my card!"

The audience erupts into applause. The woman with the shopping bags steps forward and drops two shiny quarters in front of Jack. One of the men in the suits presents Jack with a dollar. One by one, other members of the crowd bring Jack money. We did it! And we're rich!

I put my hand on my best friend's shoulder as he collects the money and the cards.

There is nothing that the Great Jackaroni and the Great Georgini can't do.

Noticing a card that's blown a little down the path, I step away from Jack. As I snatch up the card, a shadow hovers over my head, and a voice says, "Good work, kid." I straighten up and look at the speaker—who's looking right back at me.

"Oh my goodness!" I gasp. There he is: top hat, blue cape, the works! The Great Macaroni. And he can see me! The card nearly slips from my fingers as my jaw drops wide open.

"Th-th-th-thank you, sir," I manage to stutter. My heart flutters around my chest. "J-j-j-j-jack?" I say, trying to get my best friend's attention. He's too busy scooping the wet cards from the fountain. *J-j-j-j-jack,* I mouth, but the words are missing.

"You two make a great team," the Great Macaroni adds.

"Th-th-th-thanks," I manage to get out. I've given up on getting Jack's attention and instead am staring at my hero. Suddenly my eyes blur, and my head feels dizzy. As if it wasn't intimidating enough to be meeting this genius, I've just realized—"I stole your trick! I'm so sorry!"

The Great Macaroni laughs. "Please," he insists with a wave of his hand, "it's yours. You took my trick and made it your own. You're great."

My fear fades away. "It's all because of you." Remembering my best friend, I add, "And Jack."

He shakes his head. "No. It's because of you." He points at me, and I can almost feel a beam of warm-fuzzies shooting from his finger, hitting my heart, and fluttering around my insides. "You're fantastic. Don't forget it." He winks at me before turning around, leaving me alone to bask in his lingering glow.

"J-j-j-j-jack," I manage to bumble again, this time with sound. I dash over to my best friend. Fantastic. The Great Macaroni thinks I, George, am fantastic. "Jaaaaaaaaack."

Jack scoops up the last of our hard-earned money and stuffs it into his pockets. He hands me the cards. "Why don't you hold on to these?" he says, sounding much sadder than you'd think after our prize-winning performance. "To remember me—"

"Hey, Jack?" I interrupt.

"Yeah?"

"Could I have one of our coins?"

Shrugging, he says, "Sure," and hands me a penny.

I rub it around in my fingers before tossing it into the fountain. It hits the surface with a tiny plunk before slowly drifting down to the bottom. "I WISH EVERY DAY COULD BE LIKE TODAY!" I say this very loudly in case it's difficult for the Magical Fountain Folk to hear from way down beneath the water. "Right? Can you imagine? Jack and George, together forever!"

He nearly sobs in response.

My heart aches with this reply, but I understand. Jack has given me everything I've ever wanted. Even though it breaks my heart, I know what I need to do next.

"Listen, Jack," I say. "I have to show you something." Slowly, I reach into my pocket. Deep in the bottom, beneath the torn flier and the rainbow handkerchief chain, I find what I'm looking for. I gulp, feeling guilty for keeping this from him so long, especially after what he just did for me. "I forgot to give this to Uncle Chester," I say as I pull out his dad's business card and drop it into Jack's hands.

CHAPTER 31
JACK

The small paper rectangle feels heavy in my shaking hands. That fake memory thing *worked*? I was just about to let George go, but how can I now?

I skip over the phone number, since Dad won't answer anyway, and scan the rest of the card to find his address. He always used to work at home when he wasn't traveling the globe, so I'm pretty sure he's living in . . . Revere? So he *was* just a short ride away this whole time! And he never . . . I bite my lip and shake the thought from my mind. He must have an explanation, and I can't wait to hear it soon.

I yank my phone out of my pocket and plug in the address. An orange subway train, then a blue one, getting off at the Wonderland station. "Guess it wasn't Neverland, but I was pretty close," I tell George, nudging him with a laugh.

He scrunches up a very confused brow. "Huh?"

"Forget it," I say. "We need to get on a train."

He salutes. "Aye, aye, sir!"

As I'm about to stuff my phone back into my pocket, I notice the stream of missed texts from Jason:

Are you alive, man?

Yo, Jack?

Helloooo?

WTF Jack

Answer the text or I'm telling my dad.

There's one from Morgan, too: *George says he BUMPED INTO you at the store????*

I send her a blushing emoji with a quick, *Please don't tell.*

To Jason, I merely type, *I'm alive.* It's been hours since my last update. Has he told?

I see the three little dots that show he's typing, and I wait. The anticipation is horrible as they disappear and reappear and disappear again.

After several agonizing moments, his message comes through. *Not when you get home. I'm gonna kill you. Morgan and I have been freaking out.*

Morgan? Freaking out? I decide not to address that questionable statement. Instead I type, *I've almost found my dad.*

Hurry, he replies. No arguments there.

"Come on," I tell George, grabbing his hand and running toward the Orange Line subway stop just down the street.

George's magic tricks have been more useful than I even dreamed. Not only did the cash we earned buy my train ticket, I also snagged a bag of pretzels and a Coke from the vending machine before boarding.

I chow down in silence as we ride, obsessively checking the map on my phone to make sure I know the way. *Transfer at State to the Blue Line*, I repeat in my head, again and again. *Transfer at State to the Blue Line.* It's only a twenty-minute ride total, but I can't stop worrying about everything that can go wrong before we get there.

After the incident of controlling George, I'm afraid to imagine what my family is doing right now in case it actually comes true—but that doesn't stop the endless questions from bouncing around in my brain. Will Mom call Dad? Will Aunt Rachel and Uncle Dave find out I'm gone? Will Morgan's friend ruin everything? Will Morgan? My stomach lurches as I realize out loud, "We forgot the bikes!"

Every other passenger on our train turns to face me: two old men, a group of four high schoolers who smell like the entire fragrance counter at a department store, a woman wearing a surgical facemask, her phone-obsessed son, and a bookworm reading the largest novel I have ever seen. Or is that a dictionary? "Sorry," I say to them all, waving my hands as if I can push away their attention.

The train grumbles to a halt. "State Street," the muffled speaker announces. Saved by my stop.

"Come on, George," I whisper. "This is us." As we rise and approach the open door, the surgical mask lady stops me with an outstretched hand. I'm afraid she's about to grab me, but at the last moment, she seems to recall her fear of germs and stops just shy.

"Where's your family, honey?" I hear through the mask.

"Right here," George says, standing by my side and thumping his chest in some sort of display of solidarity. Her eyes almost flick in his direction.

"Wonderland," I say with a confident nod, before grabbing George's hand and yanking him off the train.

◆

As our second train pulls us closer and closer to my dad, I feel heavy. My stomach is practically empty and yet it feels like it's filled with rocks rather than half a bag of pretzels. The weight is even slowing down the train. I've only taken the Blue Line once before, when my parents took me to the beach, but I don't remember it being so endless.

At the same time, it somehow doesn't feel slow enough. This is what I've been waiting for, what I've wanted all this time, but all I can think about is the surgical mask lady's question. *Where's your family?*

George answered for me, and he's right—he is my family. But the answer that came to my head? Not *on an aimless cross-country journey ignoring her health to tour the world with her new motorcycle lover.* Not *somewhere at the other end of this too-short-to-never-visit train line, ignoring me and pretending I don't exist.* I thought of Aunt Rachel and Uncle Dave, both thinking I'm still in their house. I thought of Jason, glued to his phone as he waits for any sort of update from me. I even thought of Morgan, who maybe told her friend I was kind of okay.

I squeeze my fist, my too-long fingernails putting four tiny dents into the palm of my hand. Is it too late to turn around?

"Jack?" George asks, noticing my frustration. "Is something wrong?"

"Wonderland," the voice announces as the train rolls to a stop.

I close my eyes for a second, then open them with a small shake of my head. "No." Despite my hundred-pound stomach, I rise to my feet and lead George off the train, into the wonderland my dad calls home.

CHAPTER 32
GEORGE

Wonderland doesn't look anything like the movies. Instead of chessboards and rosebushes, there are a few small parking lots and streets littered with sand. My nostrils catch a fishy breeze in the air that reminds me of Uncle Chester's house. Jack leads me across the parking lot and down a residential street. I glance over my shoulder and spot a beach pavilion in the distance.

"That'd be perfect for our next magic show," I point out, stopping in my tracks.

"This way," Jack says, ignoring my observation and continuing in the exact opposite direction.

He has a point. I picture how far the cards might fly in the ocean breeze as Jack throws them into the air, and I remember how much trouble I encountered when accidentally littering just one poster. I can't imagine tracking down fifty-two playing cards. Fifty-four if you count the jokers, which I'm pretty sure you do when it comes to littering.

We wind down a few streets until we encounter an especially tall apartment complex.

"It says seventh floor," Jack says, craning his neck back to scan the building. He jostles the handle. The door is locked. I look on either side of the door for an Eat Me biscuit so we can shrink to the size of the keyhole and climb inside. Instead I find a trash can and a pile of unwanted grocery store circulars. As I try to think of other ways to bust down a door using magic or sheer walrus strength, it bursts open on its own, a jogger bolting through for an afternoon run.

Jack grabs the handle and we both scoot inside the lobby. A flickering light overhead illuminates a dead potted tree and a row of metal mailboxes. Discarded letters decorate the floor. Maybe it's not littering if it's inside? As Jack presses the button for the elevator, he remains suspiciously quiet. In fact, he's barely said a word since I gave him the business card that led us here.

Just as I feared. As soon as Jack finds his dad, it's "Goodbye, George."

A bell dings and the elevator door swings open. I look from Jack to the elevator to Jack, using my eyes to beg him not to get on, while using my entire heart to keep my mouth clamped shut. I know this is what he wants. What he needs. A bead of sweat drips down my cheek.

He glances at me and bites his lip. There's a message hiding behind his eyes, too, but I don't know what it means.

Since neither of us will speak, we shuffle inside the elevator. As the doors close, so too does my hope of a future with Jack. The number seven button lights up, and we begin to rise. It is now officially too late to turn around.

I laugh, looking at the dingy brown walls of the elevator. Jack gives me a puzzled glance. "This is kind of like the scene where she falls down the rabbit hole," I explain, "but they really got everything else one-hundred percent wrong."

Jack looks at me with a blank stare and blinks twice. Slowly, his lips curl in a smirk and he lets out a snort. He laughs and laughs and laughs, and I can't help but join him. In this one brief moment, it all feels normal and okay and even wonderful.

With the bell announcing the seventh floor, the

moment passes. Jack takes a deep breath as he prepares to reunite with his dad, and I take one to prepare for the hardest goodbye I keep having to make, knowing that this one will really be the last.

❖

I can barely hear the knocks standing right behind Jack, but after a few gentle taps, he pounds a little harder. Footsteps approach from the other side of the door. "Just a sec," a voice says. I know it's been a whole week since I saw his dad, but I definitely thought his voice used to be a little deeper than that. This voice almost sounds like . . . The door swings open. A woman?

She's just a little taller than Jack, in bare feet and a man's bathrobe. Her dark hair is wet, and she smells like vanilla.

"Can I help you?" she asks, evidently more than a little annoyed that her bath time was cut short.

Jack stutters, "I-I-I . . ." before trailing off.

Suddenly the woman's eyes widen in recognition. "Wait a second," she says. "You're the kid!" My eyes roll, because of course Jack's a kid. She reaches out to grab Jack's shoulders, but I get there first, pulling him back just beyond her grasp. Stranger danger! "Jack?" she asks, unsure.

How the hexagon did she know his name? "Let's get outta here!" I tell Jack.

He doesn't need to be told twice. Together we bolt down the hall. I don't look back, but I hear her bare feet thudding against the carpet behind us. "Wait!" the woman calls.

I push the elevator button, but Jack yanks me through a door lit up by a glowing red EXIT sign. We pound down the stairs. The woman stops on the landing at the top. "Come on," she calls out, her voice booming through the space. We don't come on, instead running down, down, down.

"Fudge fudge fudge fudge fudge," Jack says in between steps, but with much ruder language that I never want to hear from his lips again. As we pop out of the stairwell and into the lobby, the elevator dings open, and he and I both scream.

"Heavens!" an old woman squeals, clutching her bosom as her fluffy black dog with a wonderful gray beard barks frantically.

"Sorry," Jack says breathlessly before dashing outside the apartment complex and back toward the subway station.

We don't say anything until we're safely back on the train. "I've really ruined everything this time," he moans.

"Who was that?" I ask, not understanding any of this.

"Someone special," Jack spits, as if that explains everything. I nod but don't ask for more information because the words are clearly dripping with disgust.

Jack's phone buzzes. He pulls it out and looks at the screen. I peek over his shoulder and see the message from Jason. *I'm sorry, Jack. They know.* :(

"Fudge," Jack says, again forgetting his polite words. "And they know where we are now. They could board this train at any second."

"Maybe the lady isn't the one who told?" I suggest.

Jack shrugs. "You're right. Could've been Jason. Morgan. Their friend."

"Maybe even the gopher lady," I offer helpfully.

"God, I told everyone," he groans. "I'm so stupid."

"No you're not," I say, squeezing my friend's shoulder.

"It could even be Mom," he continues. "When we hung up, she screamed at me that if she found out I went to Daddy-O's, she would—"

"Wait," I interrupt. "She said Daddy-O's?"

Jack nods. "Kinda weird, right?"

I squeeze his shoulder harder, rocking back and forth. "Weren't you listening to anything I said?" He clearly has no idea what he's missed. "When I was listing all those restaurants?" He shakes his head again, completely lost. "Daddy-O's Beef Burger Barbecue? The one with all the cowboy hats."

Jack's mouth drops open, and he slaps himself on the forehead. "It's too late," he says, defeated.

"No, Jack," I insist. "It's not too late until they find you."

He gives me a crooked smile before looking left and right, slipping the hood of Jason's hoodie over his head, and sinking into his seat to become as invisible as possible.

I close my eyes and will my body to fade out, like now you see me, now you don't, for once under my own control. "Stick with me, Jack," I say with an invisible laugh. "I'm an expert at disappearing."

I'm quite certain nothing remains except my floating smile, and I grin even wider, realizing there's a second thing that they got right about Wonderland.

CHAPTER 33
JACK

We look up directions to Daddy-O's on my phone, and a short subway ride and brief walk later, George and I are following our server through the dimly lit restaurant. There are more horns and cowboy hats lining the walls than you could even count. We walk past a bunch of empty tables. Maybe it's kind of early for a full-sized Western meal, but the scents of bacon and garlic waft in from the kitchen.

"You can wait for your dad here," the server says, pointing to a booth.

I slide in, and George slips in right by my side.

"More room on the other side for your dad," he explains.

I nod. Twirling her pencil, the server asks, "Can I get you anything in the meantime?"

"Just my dad, please," I say politely.

"And some nachos," George adds.

The woman smiles before making her way to the only other table with customers.

"She's nice," George says.

"Mm-hmm," I answer. My fingers drum across the table. I'm so tired of waiting and running and pretending to be invisible. Let's just hope Dad doesn't answer his phone for Mom or Aunt Rachel or his someone special, either. It's my only chance that he might still walk through those tacky saloon doors.

As if on cue, the doors swing open. The butterflies in my stomach go wild as I wonder who has found me first—Mom? Dad? Dad's someone special, still wearing the robe Mom and I bought Dad for his birthday two years ago?

It's none of the above. Two not-my-dads and their small kid enter the restaurant and wait to be seated. I slink farther down in the booth. I'm so tired of thinking somebody might care.

Unaware of my rollercoaster of distress, George pushes the saltshaker across the table from one hand to the next, back and forth. With an overly forceful push, the shaker shoots past his right hand in front of me. I stop it, raising it off the table. Cupped in my hand, the saltshaker hardly weighs anything, but it's undeniably real. The Great Georgini, indeed.

My butt shifts in the booth so I'm facing George. I put the shaker down in front of him. "Can you explain this?"

My best friend's nose crinkles. "Well, if your food is bland, you turn it upside down and these little white flakes sprinkle onto—"

"Not salt," I insist. "How it moved!"

George shakes his head. "What do you mean, Jack? You saw me playing with it."

He doesn't get it. He doesn't know what he is, and I've never had the heart to tell him. Invisible, sure, but imaginary—never.

So, what is up with George and the salt shaker? George and the bike? George with a family? George the magician? He's imaginary, so how is he doing this?

I look up at him. The pepper shaker is now bouncing back and forth from one hand to the next. With a "Whoops!" he bobbles this one, too. It shoots off the table and rolls across the floor, tapping the heel of the server as she passes by.

After bending down to pick it up, she walks over to us and places it back on the table. "Be careful, pal," she says, looking at me.

"Sorry," George and I say in unison.

When she's gone, I begin again. "George, I don't understand . . ."

"He'll be here soon," my friend reassures me, although that's not what I'm talking about.

It's like he's creating a new George. A real one. An even cooler version than I could have ever imagined.

As if I don't have enough to worry about, the gopher lady's warning replays in my mind. *Let him go, or he'll disappear forever.*

I can't let him disappear. Even if I can't keep him with me, George is too good for the world to lose. He feels so real right now—but will he when my dad comes through that door? How much longer can I really hold on to him?

My eyes are watering for like the hundredth time today. I can't even look at George, so instead I pull out my phone. It hasn't stopped buzzing since Jason said we were busted. I flick through the messages and missed calls. Aunt Rachel. Uncle Dave. Aunt Rachel. Aunt Rachel. Morgan. Jason. Uncle Dave.

The screen lights up as another message arrives: *Jack, honey, please answer. We're worried sick. You're not in trouble. Just please talk to us.*

I'm literally shaking, inside and out. Mom and

Dad left me without looking back. I leave Aunt Rachel for two seconds and she's begging me to come home.

What have I done?

"We have to go," I say to George. I toss the rest of our magic trick money onto the table to tip the server for seating us and crawl over George to get out of the booth. He rises behind me, and together we scurry through the door and race down the sidewalk.

"Jaaaack, wait!" George calls, trailing behind.

"I can't stay here," I pant over my shoulder as I run. I need to get home.

But first I need to get back to the Bath Stuff and Such—probably a fifteen-minute walk away—where I left the bikes. Maybe, *maybe* if I can get those bikes back to the garage and slink up the stairs and slip under the covers of the blow-up mattress, I can pretend I've been in bed this whole time. That this whole "missing Jack" commotion woke me up from a deep sleep. I can pretend I never met Dad's someone special. That I never learned about Mom's motorcycle man. That I never hurt my aunt and uncle.

"Can we not-stay-here a little more slowly?" George asks, beginning to huff and puff. "We walruses are not known for our on-land speed."

I stumble to a halt. If I want to hurry, I can't take him with me. This is it.

"Listen, George. I have to go back to Aunt Rachel and Uncle Dave's where I belong," I begin, my arm shaking as I gesture to my chest. "And you," I add, now pointing to him with my wobbly rubber arms, "need to find a better friend than me."

His mouth drops open. "There's no such thing," he insists, shaking his head. "I need you, Jack, and you need me. At least until you find your dad! Your aunt and uncle don't—"

"They're my family," I choke out, "and it's important for family to stick together."

"But what about your parents?"

I pause. What about my parents? Mom's sick, or so they tell me, but that doesn't mean it's okay that she left me. And don't even get me started on Dad. He's a mystery. But after all that, after everybody leaving, the way Aunt Rachel and Uncle Dave took me in, and Jason covered for me, and Morgan, well, let's leave Morgan out of this. The point is: I have to go back. Finally, I tell George, "It's important for family to stick together even when some of 'em don't." I reach out to him and put my hand on his arm.

"I'm your family, too." His voice trembles, and he's using the big bulging sad-walrus-calf eyes that could break any heart if only it weren't already so broken. "Let's run away together. We can have a great adventure. We can have millions of adventures. Walruses. Magic tricks. Pirates. Vampires. Escalators!" His voice is scratchy and his eyes flood with water, as he adds hopefully, "Tree houses?"

I shake my head. "I want all of those adventures for you, George. Every single one. But they can't be with me. There are so many people out there who need a friend like you—"

"Nobody else even sees me," George fights back. "There's just one." His mustache flares with each sniff as he unsuccessfully tries to suppress his tears. I realize that I've never imagined him crying before.

"That's what I used to think too. But George, you're different now. That kid in the park saw you. And the gopher."

"And the Great Macaroni," George adds with a sniff.

"Well okay, then!" I say. "And when you were with me, all that time ago, it was just me. How boring was that? Find someone new. Because your job here is done. You saved me." This last sentence would've been a lot more convincing if I didn't release a snot-and-tear-filled blubber as the words came out. "Trust me. You need to find someone new or else—" I stop, unable to speak the horrible fate that awaits George if he doesn't move on from me, and fast.

"I'll disappear. Forever."

My insides slosh as I nod.

"Please, Jack. I'm your best friend."

"You were," I correct, even though deep down, I know it's still true. He's trying so hard, and it's almost working. I have to stop this. I shake my head, unsure what else to say to make this end. To make this pain disappear. "But that doesn't matter anymore. It's not real."

His eyes nearly pop out of his head. "What's not real?" he asks.

"This friendship." I look over my shoulder in what I assume is the direction of Aunt Rachel's house. "The gopher lady." Desperate to get him to understand, I add a soft "You."

There's a tiny gasp. George's arms are shaking. They flicker twice.

"Not real for *me*," I frantically try to explain. "Anymore. But for someone else—"

"Well, Jack," he interrupts, sounding unusually formal. His lips are quivering, but he keeps his tone steady. "I guess I should go." His shoulders slink, and he turns away. I want to shout *Wait,* but I know I can't. I watch him shuffle down the sidewalk.

A minute passes. I'm tired and hungry, and I need to go home. His silhouette gets smaller and smaller. My tears really start to stream when I remember Mom dumping me on Aunt Rachel's front lawn. She said it was for the best, and maybe she was right, but that doesn't mean it didn't crush me. Now in trying to save George, I've hurt him as much as Mom ever hurt me. I can't win. "This isn't fair!" I cry out to nobody, because nobody real's around. How do I fix this?

"Blaaaaargh," I cry out, before yanking out my cell phone.

There's only half a ring before Uncle Dave is on the line. "JACK!" he cries out. He is out of breath. "Are you okay?"

"I'm fine." I can't even see George in the distance. I don't have time to answer all Uncle Dave's questions.

"Where are you, buddy? Why did you run away? Are you sure you're okay?"

I hear a "Let me talk to him!" on the other end of the phone. I smile at Jason's enthusiasm but I *really* don't have time for that.

"Listen, Uncle Dave. I'm fine. I have to do one thing. Then I'll head home."

I'm about to hang up when he insists, "Wait! Where are you going, Jack? I have to tell Rachel. Please." He has that shaky sound in his voice, the same one that he had when Morgan fell out of that tree, and we all had to wait in the hospital. It's his scared parent voice, and I'm not even *his* kid.

My eyes get all watery again. Man, I'm such a baby. "I'm sorry," I sniff. "I'm so sorry."

And suddenly, I know exactly where George is going. "I just have to help a friend. Then you can come get me. Please. I'll be at the—" My phone buzzes as the screen lights up briefly and powers off. The battery is dead.

CHAPTER 34
GEORGE

"Zoo discount," I remind the bus security camera as I walk past without paying. With each row I pass, I hope to find the mysterious gopher lady, but no such luck. She'd just say "I told you so" anyway, so it's probably for the best.

The bus begins to move, and I almost fall over in the aisle. I tuck into a row before I can make a fool of myself. Not that anybody would notice. I'm still flickering in and out, but I haven't disappeared, which is a good sign, I guess.

"He said I'm not real," I complain to nobody in particular. My heart refuses to believe it, but if I really think about it . . . being ignored, walked through, forgotten, magic. I'm such a fool. A teardrop drips from my eye and plunks onto my hand.

I raise my wrist to examine the wet dot. It certainly looks real to me.

I think back over the past few days, and all the times that our friendship wasn't real. That I haven't mattered. When I hid a voicemail from Jack. When I lost sight of his mom at the airport and let her get away. When I brought Jack face-to-face with a woman in a bathrobe, who is somehow both special and terrible. When I ruined the *Alice in Wonderland* franchise. When I took Jack to a restaurant that provided us with neither his dad nor my nachos. When I pulled Jack away from his aunt and uncle even though he clearly wanted to stay with them.

My vision blurs in and out for a moment. The bus becomes suddenly cartoony and there's a floppy mop man by my side. "Hey, George is back!" he cries out. A few rows up, a gopher lady lookalike peeks over the seat, smiling as she sees me. I'm sure she wasn't there a moment ago.

Her name returns to me. "Miranda?" I close and rub my eyes. When I open them again, I'm back on the regular bus. The mop and gopher lookalike are gone.

"What was that?" I wonder aloud. I shake it from my mind because, like me, it doesn't even matter.

My thoughts return to Jack. Now that's a guy who matters. Everyone's looking for him and he didn't even have to make his own fliers.

A woman with wonderfully large hair and movie-star sunglasses takes the spot directly beside me. Her bag falls to my feet. A perfectly painted pink finger reaches up and taps a piece of plastic looped over her ear. It's exactly like the headset Jack gave to me when he whisked me away to the airport. After a moment, she says, "Hello?"

She's either on the phone or asking her invisible friend to spy on her mom. Sometimes it's hard to tell, but I'm going to pretend she's talking to me so I don't feel so horribly alone.

"Hi," I respond. "George Odobenidae." I tip the hat I wish I had.

"I heard what happened," she says. "I am so sorry. And I know you don't want to hear this right now, but you'll find someone else, sweetie."

Okay. I'm a little freaked that this woman's words actually match my situation with Jack. It almost makes me feel like our friendship *was* real.

I rescan the events of the past week, and I think I catch a few brief moments where I really did matter. When I cleaned Jack's mom's room. When I helped get Jack some fruit because he was hungry. When I made Jack laugh every time I thought he was about to cry. When I wowed the world with my magic. When the Great Macaroni said that I was fantastic.

Jack didn't know what he was talking about. Should I go back and tell him?

"Don't do anything you'll regret," my seat buddy warns whoever she's talking to on her earpiece. "You know he'll only hurt you again."

I've never had a more two-sided one-sided conversation before. This is totally spooky. "You're not giving Jack enough credit," I say, still imagining that she's actually talking to me. "I don't think he wanted to hurt me. I think he was trying to help. He said I saved him. He said my job was done. He practically begged me to find someone else." That's got to mean something, right?

"Hon, it sounds to me like he has you all mixed up. Maybe you need to take a beat to focus on yourself, on who you want to be, before you worry about him or finding someone else."

Maybe she's right. The *Have you seen this person?* poster crinkles in my pocket as I shift in my seat. Maybe I don't need other people to see me to tell me who I am. To prove that I'm important.

With that, the flickering stops. I'm whole again. "Thank you," I say, patting my new friend on the hand. "And I know you can't hear me, but you matter, too."

The bus driver announces, "Zoo stop."

I climb over my seatmate's bag and stumble into the aisle. "Well, it was nice pretending to talk to you," I tell her over my shoulder.

"Go get 'em, George Odobenidae," she replies.

My bulgy eyes twitch as I whip my head around to face her. "You can see me?"

But the seat is empty.

"What the phantom?!" I exclaim. The lady has disappeared, and I almost wonder, as I climb off the bus, if she was ever even there.

CHAPTER 35
JACK

B ath Stuff and Such is in the opposite direction from the zoo, but getting to the zoo on foot would be impossible, and I'm all out of bus money. Once I've got Jason's bike and I'm almost back to where I began, sirens sound in the distance. My legs pedal harder. *Not yet, Uncle Dave. I have to get to George first.*

As soon as they find me, I'm in huge trouble. No zoo for me ever again, even if my best friend needs me.

And yes, I know. After all I've done, I deserve it. But he deserves better.

I can't pedal fast enough yet somehow, I'm pedaling too fast. When a pigeon crosses in front of me, the next thing I know, I'm tumbling sideways onto the grass. I rub my arms and my freshly grass-stained elbows.

A car pulls up to the side of the road and comes to a stop as I push myself up. I get ready to run, but I'm stopped by a "Jack?"

My heart freezes. I whip around and cannot believe who I see. "Dad?" He's scruffier than the last time I saw him. I race toward him, the person I've been looking for this whole time. He catches me in a hug that would look great in a movie. I press my face into his chest to hide the fact that I'm sobbing. I can't stop the tears. "Where did you—?" I sniff. "How did you—?"

Dad's sniffling and snorting, too, and asking the same kind of questions: "How could you—? Why did you—?" I feel tiny tears plonking down on my neck, but I don't brush them off.

"Jack," he says finally, "I've got to call Rachel and Dave. Wait here?" I hesitate before letting go. I've seen this trick before. I watch very carefully to make sure he doesn't slip away as he gets into the car and pulls out his phone. He punches the numbers, and I read his lips: "I found him." So, his phone does work.

When I'm positive he won't sneak away, I turn to study the scene. I want to remember this forever as the time and place I found my dad. I notice the grass, blowing in the summer breeze. The pigeon I nearly smooshed waddles around farther down the sidewalk, waiting to trip the next innocent kid who rushes by. I look at the building closest to me, and I feel the color drain from my face: Daddy-O's Beef Burger Barbeque. Exactly where George said I'd find my dad. He was right.

Somewhere in the distance, a church bell bongs once. It's one o'clock. Exactly when George said Dad would be here.

My eyes refill with water as I think of my best friend, the one I just crushed if not destroyed. The best friend who was right the whole time. The most real best friend I've ever had.

I can't let that awful conversation be our last. Even if I need to let him go, I have to say goodbye the right way. I have to let him know how much he means to me, how much he helped me. I have to tell him how much the world needs a friend like the Great Georgini.

Dad's still on the phone with Aunt Rachel, or is he calling someone else now? Either way, he doesn't seem to be looking at me. I walk over to Jason's bike, pick it up, and hop on. Sorry, Dad.

"Hey! Where do you think you're going?" Dad's

voice calls out, as the car door slams shut. I hear his feet on the pavement as he runs up behind me. A moment later he's hoisting me off the bike. He sets me down, reaches under my chin, and unsnaps the helmet. With the accompanying *click*, I realize I'm running out of options. "Get in the car," he says, turning me around to face the passenger door.

I don't move. All I can picture is George: lost, alone, and thinking he doesn't matter. Maybe even disappearing or worse. I can't just abandon him without making sure he's going to be okay. I look at Dad. I'm not like him.

"I can't," I say, crossing my arms.

Dad has picked up the bike and is carrying it toward the back of his car. He scoots around me, clicking the trunk open with his keychain. "What do you mean you can't?" he asks.

"I'm not going home. I have to help someone."

As he closes Jason's bike into the trunk, he looks up. "Oh yeah?" he asks. "And who's that?"

"George."

Dad smiles as he approaches me. "Jack," he begins, kneeling in front of me. "Let's go home." He puts his hand on my shoulder.

"If we go home, you'll stay there?" I ask hopefully.

His smile droops into a frown. He doesn't answer, but the expression says it all.

"I'm going to the zoo," I tell him, pushing his hand off my shoulder. "Now are you going to take me, or do I have to walk?"

Dad shrugs. "Jack," he begs. "You know he's not re—"

"Please, Dad," I say desperately. "I left Aunt Rachel's to find you, and now I've lost George because of it. He told me he'd take me to you because you couldn't even stop in to say hello, so I followed him all over town, and now you're here. Exactly where he said you'd be."

Dad doesn't answer.

I continue, "It's because of George, and now I've got to thank him because here you are and here I am, and that's all I ever wanted to begin with." I pull out the heart-wrenching begging walrus eyes that I've learned from George. "Please. Don't you believe me?"

Dad looks away. "If I take you to the zoo, you'll let me take you home after?"

I nod, and he sighs.

"All right," he finally agrees. "Get in the car."

I race to the car, throwing the door open and

leaping inside. Dad is slower. *Hurry up,* I command him with my mind. The trick doesn't work, but I'm not the magician in the family.

I snap my seatbelt across my chest, and it's a good thing I do. I'm practically jumping off the seat with excitement. Dad and I, together at last, and on our way to George. The car grumbles to a start when Dad turns the key. "You're next, Mom," I whisper. "You're next."

CHAPTER 36
GEORGE

The zoo is more crowded today. I weave between the crowd as I make my way to the entrance and push my way through the turnstile.

"Yo, kid!" the gatekeeper calls out behind me. I wonder who's getting yelled at now, but I don't have time to care.

"Uncle Chester!" I call over the fence when I get to the walrus exhibit, waving my arms over my head. When he doesn't respond, I bite my lip. He's probably hurt that I left for so long without calling. Family sticks together, so here I am. The Odobenidaes, together again, if only I can get to them. People who matter don't disappear through doors.

I look to either side of me. A zookeeper in a tan uniform is telling a small group of parents and kids some interesting facts about walruses. I remember most of them from reading the plaque last time and from my online searches. He's too busy to give me the keys, and I'm too invisible for him to give them to, anyway.

I take a deep breath, and then one more. I've never liked heights, but it looks like over the fence is my best option. Here goes nothing. I hoist my feet off the ground a few inches, before sinking back down to the pavement. This is going to be harder than I thought.

Maybe if I get a running start? I take ten steps back before making a running leap at the fence. I'm flying for a moment, until my waist hits the top of the glass fence and I bend in the middle. The next thing I know, I'm sliding back down onto the pavement.

Two girls giggle by my side. The younger of the two gapes at me with her mouth wide open.

"You can see me?" I ask.

Before they can answer, a voice honks from behind them: "Young man." There is a not-so-subtle hint of warning in his tone.

"Me?" I crane my neck to find a rather large blue penguin wedged between the girls. He wears a tan outfit that matches the one the zookeeper tour guide has. Another weirdo like the mysterious gopher lady and Stanley the alien.

"Feet on the grrrrrrrround," he squawks.

"Sir, yes, sir," I salute, smiling widely. Nobody's ever scolded me like that before. I just hope my uncle Chester was watching. Would somebody who doesn't matter get scolded by a penguin who clearly does? I don't think so!

Hey, wait a second. A bossy penguin at the zoo in tacky khaki. He must be an employee! My eyes dart down to his waist. There is a ring hooked to his belt loop with thousands of official-looking keys. Recalling the Employees Only entrance that leads to Chester's exhibit, I smile my very sweetest smile and ask the penguin for a favor.

❖

"Thank you, Weatherby!" From inside the exhibit, I wave to my newfound penguin friend as he waddles away, keys jingling with each flop of his flippers. Wanda and Wendla are draped across some rocks. As for Uncle Chester, he's decided to take a dip in the early afternoon sun.

I cautiously kneel at the water's edge, unsure

how he'll react to my return. It's been days since he's heard from me. Slowly, I lean forward and poke my head beneath the surface. With a forceful snort, bubbles shoot from my nostrils and surprisingly, this time, they sound like jingling bells. *I'm home,* I ring to Uncle Chester.

I wait. My eyes open. At the far end of the pool, I spot Chester, like a graceful two-thousand-pound mermaid. He remains silent, so I keep going. "Ring-a-ling-a-ling," my nostrils say, which translates beautifully to, *Jack needed me. And I kind of needed him. Did you know I matter?*

Still nothing.

I lift my head above the surface and gasp for air. I've got a lot of walrus practice ahead of me if I'm ever going to have a full conversation with Uncle Chester in one sitting. I suck in one last breath before sticking my head underwater again. *I don't want you to take it personally, er, walrusally, that I was gone so long,* my nose bubbles say. *I got a little lost along the way.*

I recall the flier, still stuffed in my back pocket. *Have you seen this person?* With a great deal of difficulty, my left hand reaches into my pocket while my right one props me up and stops me from falling headfirst into the water. Once I've grasped the torn poster, I tug it out and stick it under the water. *See?* my nose tinkles. The paper begins to dissolve and float away. Oh no!

But finally, I hear a tiny tingling. *You back for good?*

For good and for bad, I chime back playfully, thinking of all the mischief I can get into running around the zoo.

Uncle Chester makes a sharp turn underwater and begins to swim toward me. It's less graceful and more terrifying when the rather large being is heading directly for you. I want to flinch and pull my head out of the water, but I don't. Instead I brace myself for impact. Please don't hurt. Please don't hurt.

Just as we're about to collide, he comes to a perfectly timed stop. We are nose to nose. His soulful bulgy eyes look directly into mine. We both refuse to blink, and time stands still for a moment. All I hear is the splash of the water lapping against the rocks.

Chester inches forward ever so slightly. Our noses tap. I can feel his magnificent mustache against mine as he nuzzles me. He missed me, too.

I don't think you can cry while underwater, which is a good thing because my tears would overflow this pool and drown the entire zoo.

Finally, I'm home.

With an impressive heave, Uncle Chester pulls himself onto the rocks as I lift my head, opening my mouth to take in as much sweet, sweet air as possible. I roll my eyes as I notice one half of my drenched, disintegrating flier has found Uncle Chester, clinging to his side. "And this is why we don't litter," I groan. I rip the damp paper off my uncle's crackly skin. The now-upside-down drawing of the lost, lonely boy looks exactly like . . . I frown . . . Jack?

I look at Chester, thinking of how much one small gesture changed everything.

I close my eyes, wishing for that kind of change for Jack more than anything.

CHAPTER 37
JACK

Dad stares straight ahead at the trees and passing cars. I don't know what to say. Afraid that anything will send him running again. Almost afraid he's not even real.

"Why did you run away, Jack?" Dad asks, finally breaking the silence and briefly glancing in my direction.

"No," I reply. "You first." I may only have this ride with Dad before he zips off to Wonderland or Neverland or Loch Ness, and I'm pretty sure everyone will be asking me his questions once I'm home. It is *my* turn. "Where were you, Dad? Nine months and I never got to see you even once. You barely even called me. And suddenly, Mom's gone and you're telling answering machines that you wanted me this whole time? 'Cause that's a messed-up way to show it." I think I may be shouting. I've never yelled at my dad before. It doesn't feel right, but I also can't stop. *"Why did you leave me?"*

He keeps his eyes on the road, refusing to look at me. "Listen, Jack," he begins, "your mother and I, we were explosive." He chuckles to himself as he thinks back to some memory I never want to hear. "In a lot of ways. But when you hit a certain age, the impulses, the unpredictability, they're not fun anymore. They're just pathetic. I was miserable."

"How do you think Mom feels?" I ask. "Aunt Rachel said Mom can't control these things. She says Mom's sick."

Dad breathes in through his nose. He doesn't have to say anything because his nostrils have said it all. He knows. He knew then, and he left anyway. The terror creeping into the crevices around his eyes is not for Mom's sake. It's for his. He's busted.

Dad finally responds, "She's a trooper."

Now I know I'm yelling: "Mom was on the couch for three weeks after you left. She barely moved. I cooked her dinner. I walked myself to school. I told everyone else she—*we* were fine. When Aunt Rachel called, I told her Mom was out running errands or seeing her friends so she wouldn't worry. But at least Aunt Rachel bothered to check in. Where were you when we were *trooping*? You were supposed to be taking care of ME. To be MY DAD! But you didn't care at all!"

Dad is stunned. "I didn't know."

"You didn't know you're supposed to be my father?" I sound like Morgan's friend George after seeing a phone that's more than six months old.

"I didn't know she'd be depressed."

Depressed. Is that what Aunt Rachel was talking about? My eyes sting as the tears finally spill. She wasn't just sad; she was *depressed*, and I didn't even know it. I'm such an idiot. I glare up at my Dad. What's his excuse? "How could you just disappear?"

He runs his fingers through his hair. It's thinner than I remember. When he finally speaks, his voice is as broken as mine. "I messed up, Jacky."

I nod. I already knew that, but it's nice to hear somebody else admit it for a change. "Then fix it."

His Adam's apple lurches as if he's going to be physically ill. "Your mother and I are not getting back together."

"I'm not talking about that." At least I'm not

the only fool in the family. "What about me? You think you can just run off and find a new family, and the old one doesn't matter? Yeah, Mom is tough. A trooper. But she needs help. Maybe you can't handle that. Fine. But don't go around calling Mom the pathetic one, because she is not pathetic. She's sick, and she's having a hard time, but she's trying, and she's here, Dad." I pause for a moment as I recall the past week. "Mostly," I add quietly.

I'm no longer crying. I've shed too many tears for him. I make sure he's looking at me when I demand again: "Why. Did. You. Leave. Me?"

"Jack, I never intended—"

"Tell me!" I command.

"BECAUSE IT WAS EASY," he bursts out.

His words feel like a slap in the face. "Oh. I get it," I whisper, looking down toward the cup holder between us so he doesn't have to look at the pain in my eyes. It'll be easier for him this way.

Dad pulls over and clicks on the flashers. As the lights *tick-tick-tick-tick-tick*, he takes off his seatbelt so he can turn to face me. With an outstretched hand, he gently lifts my chin. Our eyes meet. The brown speckles in his remind me remarkably of George's in this light. Silent tears stream down his face.

"Jaaaack," he softly says, his tone begging me to understand.

"Avoiding me is easy." I sniff, amused as I realize something. "And you know what, Dad? That's why I ran away from Aunt Rachel's. Because it was easy. Because I'm pathetic. Because I'm more like you than I thought. But I was going to go back to Aunt Rachel's after I help my friend. Where would *you* be if George hadn't convinced me to run away?"

Dad is blubbering, tears streaming. He takes a deep, shaky breath. "I'm here now, buddy." He reaches over and drapes his arm around me. I nestle in, sniffling and snorting, but still not finding any more tears for him. The scent of his ocean wind deodorant takes me back to a time before he left. He's here, and maybe that's enough. For now.

After a few moments of our synchronized sniffing, Dad turns the key and pulls back onto the road. With a shaky voice, he asks, "You want to explain this George thing now?"

Where to begin? Disappearing. Reappearing. The gopher lady. Family. Magic tricks. "It's like he's creating a new George, and this one's real."

"That's impossible, Jack," Dad corrects me. "*You're* creating a new George."

"Maybe," I admit, "but I can't ride two bikes." Dad doesn't understand. "He gave me your business card, too. So that coffee thing was real?"

"What coffee thing?" Dad glances at me, shaking his head. "Jack, I packed you a—"

"Thanks for telling him I was at Aunt Rachel's, by the way."

My Dad's arms prickle with goosebumps that remind me of George's bumpy skin. "How did you know?"

"How come you could see him, Dad, and nobody else?"

"I didn't see him. I . . ." Dad trails off. "I just kind of sensed him. It seemed like a piece of you was there, so I went with it. I guess I wanted to believe in it. Believe in you."

That's the nicest thing he's said to me since before he left.

Brightly colored banners with pictures of monkeys and emus and giraffes catch my eye outside. We're here.

"I just need to find a place to park," Dad says.

I groan. The lot is packed. I don't see an open spot anywhere. This is gonna take forever. My heart is hammering. I can't take the suspense as we drive around and around and around. We're wasting time!

When Dad comes to a stop, looking left and right for an empty spot, I unbuckle my seatbelt.

"What are you doing?" he says, his serious voice returning.

"Just meet me inside. George needs me!"

"Jack, get back here!"

But I'm already out of the car and racing across the parking lot. I hope I'm not in too much trouble for this. Like it really matters—I mean, I already ran away. How much is bolting out of Dad's car really going to add to my punishment?

As I arrive at the front gate, I leap over a turnstile like an action hero. The ticket vendor watches me with an open mouth. I hope it looks like slow-motion from over there.

"Hey you!" she shouts as I land. "Kid!"

There's no time to stop. When a best friend is in trouble, you can't wait for anything, especially when you don't have the fourteen-dollar admission fee. I pop up onto my feet and am off. "George!" I shout, passing a tower of giraffes and a band of gorillas. "George!" I'm sure the zoo security will be on me in a second, so I run a little faster. Penguins. Polar bears. Walruses. Freeze.

"George!"

I put my hands at the top of the glass and peer into the pen. Sure enough, George is sitting on a rock next to a particularly large walrus.

"George!" I shout again, hoping he'll hear.

He doesn't.

I look to the left and to the right. Nothing else to do but pull my body up the glass and swing my leg around. I'm going in.

I hoist myself up. The water is farther down than I thought, but if I creep along this ledge right inside the fence, I should be able to—

"What are you doing?!" a lady shouts, while a man shrieks.

Somebody behind me reaches for my leg. It tickles me and catches me off guard. As I flinch away from the stranger, my leg slips off the ledge.

Bad idea, Jack.

Tumbling head over heels, I shout, "Geoooor—"

That's all I get out before I hit the water and the world turns blue.

CHAPTER 38
GEORGE

Jack is in the water. I have to save him.

"I'll be right back," I tell Uncle Chester. He swats a fly in response. With that, I'm bounding down the rocks and diving into the water. Jack's frantically splashing. He's pretty good at floating, but he's too panicked to even tread water properly.

Jack's intrusion is not making Wendla happy. She plops into the water and starts swimming toward him with an expression I can only describe as stormy.

"Remain calm," a grown-up voice instructs from above.

"I'll try," I call back, "but it's hard when your best friend's in danger!" My clothes cling to my skin like a flier to the side of a walrus. I kick harder to fight through this added weight, finally reaching Jack's flailing limbs. "Jack!"

He looks at me with wide eyes. His arms circle wildly to keep him above water. In between gasps of air, he calls out, "I can't swim, George." His mouth fills with water, and he begins to choke.

"But I can." He seems less impressed and more scared for his life. A brilliant idea flashes into my mind. "Jack," I cry out, leaning my head back to avoid taking in any water, "Just like at the fountain. Follow my instructions. Do what I do, and together, we will get through this." I make a frog-like stroke with my arms in the water, then another with my legs. I circle Jack twice, while Wendla swims a larger lap around both of us. "Got it?" I ask.

Jack watches, nods, then lunges for me. His arms wrap around my shoulders, pulling me down. "Jack!" I call, out, but it comes out more like "Ja-a-a-a-a-a-blurgle-blurgle-blurgle," because my head is underwater. My own limbs thrash about, and I force him off of me.

I pop back up above the surface, gasping. Jack reaches out to grab me again, but I pull back. If he brings me down, we're both goners. "Keep treading water, Jack," I tell him.

Jack flails sloppily. His technique could be better, but at least he's staying afloat.

"I want you to look at me. Focus." My wide eyes dart behind him to where Wendla is making a horrible fuss swimming circles around us. "Hey, did you know a female walrus is called a cow?"

He opens his mouth to speak, but again it fills with water. He chokes instead. I did not know such a time existed, but it seems this may not be the time for walrus fun facts.

"You can call her Wendla," I continue. "And she's a friend of Uncle Chester's, which means she's okay. You are okay. I will not let anything hurt you." I sound so calm for somebody who's just been nearly drowned that I almost believe me. "I'll help you," I promise.

No more ideas, George, I imagine he's thinking. *That's what got us here in the first place.*

I continue: "We can do this, Jack. You just have to trust me. Don't you believe in me?"

My question melts his fears. He nods, and I can't help getting a warm fuzzy feeling in my chest. I might even be blushing. "Then let's do this, Jack."

I look above. People are bumbling about, but nobody's doing anything useful. Grown-ups. Good grief.

Come on. Think, George. Think. Maybe I can't teach Jack to swim like I can teach him to be magic, but there's got to be a life vest around here, right? Rope? Anything? I know I can't hold him up, but if I could just help him get over to the side of the pool . . .

A flash of brown catches my eye. Wendla is getting closer with each lap. I'm pretty sure walruses don't eat humans, but Wendla might make an exception for an intruding stranger.

I push myself down beneath the surface and snort to Wendla, *This is my friend. Leave him alone.* She doesn't answer.

Swimming is getting harder by the moment. My full pockets are weighing me down.

Hey, wait a second! That's it! I can use my magic after all!

Still kicking my legs, I dig one hand into my pocket and begin pulling out the cards. They float to the surface and swim around me like little fish. They're not what I want, though. Squashed way at the bottom, I reach what I'm looking for: the rainbow chain of magic handkerchiefs.

"Take this!" I say, forcing one end into Jack's hand. "Hold on to it, and keep treading water."

Holding the other end of the chain, I swim to the shore, where I hop onto the rocks. The chain of magic handkerchiefs trails out behind me into the water, connecting me to Jack. I stuff my end under Uncle Chester to keep it secure. He grunts but doesn't move.

"Okay, Jack. Now kick!" Planting my feet on the rocks, I pull on the makeshift rope, slowly reeling Jack in. The magic handkerchiefs stretch but hold firm. My arms are still exhausted from my lifting earlier, but with Jack's kicking and my pulling, it's working.

As Jack gets closer and closer to dry land, Wendla never takes her bulgy eyes off of him. "You know you could help us?" I scold her, but she doesn't respond.

When he reaches the rock, I give him my hand. Jack climbs up before collapsing onto his stomach.

Josie the zookeeper runs across the stones to reach us.

"It's about time," I tell her.

She rolls Jack onto his back.

"George?" Jack coughs.

"Yeah?"

He tries to prop himself up on his elbows.

"Stay down, kid," the zookeeper says.

"George," Jack mumbles again.

"Your name's George?" Josie asks.

He shakes his head. "No." He points at me. "His."

The zookeeper turns to face me and nods.

"And I want him to know," Jack says, sputtering a bit, "that he matters."

I blush and look at my best friend in the whole wide world. "Thanks." Smirking in the most Jack-like way I know, I add, "You do, too, pal."

CHAPTER 39
JACK

Once the zookeeper has checked me for injuries, I'm led into a long, dark hallway. The cage door to the exhibit clanks closed behind us. In front of us, I find more zookeepers and security guards, plus Dad and Uncle Dave and Aunt Rachel and Jason and Morgan. There's crying and hugging, and it's all just a big emotional mess. Nobody gives me a hard time for risking my life and worrying them to death. They all just seem relieved that I'm okay. I apologize anyway.

Dad leans in and gives me a searching look. "Did you at least, uh, get to say what you needed to say? To George?"

I nod. "He's gonna be okay."

"Jack . . ." The voice comes from off to one side,

almost a whisper, but its familiarity cuts through all the rest of the noise.

"Mom?"

She's hovering a few feet away, looking like she hasn't slept in days. I take a soaking, shaky step toward her. Then another. My stride gets faster until I find myself wrapped in her arms.

"I'm sorry," I say. "I'm drenched."

Through a sob, she points to the giant wet spot my hug has left behind on her shirt. "Me too." We laugh.

"I'm sorry," she whispers as her knees buckle, and she slides onto the ground. I slip down with her and nestle into her arms. She strokes my head. "I'm so sorry. My sweetie. My baby. I'm so sorry." Her breaths become more strained through her tears. She's almost gasping, and still she won't stop apologizing.

I raise my hand and wave Aunt Rachel over. She quickly approaches, followed by Dave and, a little farther behind, Dad. "She needs some air," Rachel says. I lift my head from Mom's lap and step back as my aunt gets closer.

"No, no. Jacky! Jack. No!" Mom cries, grasping at the air to reach me.

"I'm right here, Mom." I reach my hand out, allowing the tips of our fingers to touch.

"It's okay, Ronnie. Jack's okay," Rachel promises. "And you will be too. I called your doctor. She can fit you in this afternoon." She drapes an arm across my shoulder. "Now let's go home."

◆

We walk to Uncle Dave's minivan together in silence. Mom keeps her eyes down and seems too exhausted to talk more. Aunt Rachel drapes a supportive arm around Mom's waist, keeping her steady.

"So," Dad says after he's loaded Jason's bike into the minivan's trunk.

I look at him. At the others. "Now what?"

Aunt Rachel shoots Uncle Dave a message using their secret eye language, as Jason and Morgan climb into the back of the van.

Aunt Rachel breaks the silence: "Jack, your mother's going to need some time." She seems to be speaking both for and with my mom.

"One week?" I ask, bracing myself for this familiar line.

"What? No!" Aunt Rachel assures me. "She's not leaving again."

Mom, still silent, draws a little cross on her heart.

"Time to heal. Time to adjust her medication. Time for therapy," Rachel continues. "And we want her—both of you—to stay with us while she gets better."

Dad's hand settles onto my shoulder as he asks, "Is that what you want, Jack? Because I could also . . ." He looks up at Aunt Rachel and Uncle Dave. He almost looks at Mom, but his eyes turn back to me before they reach hers.

Does he really want me now?

I wrap my arms around Dad, pulling him into a hug. I've been looking for him all this time, and I've finally found him. And sure, he messed up, big time, but he took me to the zoo. He brought me to George. Which means there's hope. Which means he believes in me.

Uncle Dave clears his throat. I release Dad and look from Mom to Aunt Rachel to Uncle Dave to Dad, but none of them tell me what to do. I'm not usually the decider. Finally, I take Dad's hand. "You'll come visit?" I ask him quietly.

Dad smiles and nods, before pulling me into another hug.

"Dad," I whisper into his ear, "don't disappear. Not again."

"I won't."

From inside the car, Morgan taps on the window and tells me to hurry up, but the rest of us ignore her. I just got Dad back and now I'm leaving him, but somehow it feels different this time. "Promise you'll come see me soon?"

"I promise." He straightens up and slides open the minivan's side door for me. "Promise you won't do any more high-dives into a tank full of walruses?"

I climb in. "Sorry, Dad. I can't promise that," I tease.

With a chuckle, he steps back. "Take care, buddy. Love you." As I buckle up, Mom climbs in next to me, and I think I catch a nod between Mom and Dad.

I look to Jason and Morgan in the back row. I mimic texting. "I'm alive," I say to Jason with an apologetic shrug that I stuff with gratitude.

He playfully whacks my arm. "Yeah, barely. Jeez, Jack." He's grinning, relieved and happy to see me.

From the moment that Uncle Dave starts the car until we're exiting the parking lot, I wave to my dad. He waves back, not moving a step.

Mom clutches my arm the whole way home, like she's afraid to let go. Afraid to lose me. She's still shaking.

Morgan finally breaks the silence. "Where's my bike?"

Whoops. I shrink into the seat. "Outside the Bath Stuff and Such, I guess," I say.

"Daaaaaaad," Morgan whines.

Uncle Dave looks at us in the rearview mirror. "It's fine," he says to Morgan. "We'll get it." The car turns around and heads toward Morgan's bike.

"Why'd you take it, anyway?" she asks.

"I didn't," I tell her.

"What do you mean you didn't?" she snaps. "It's missing. You know where it is."

Jason rolls his eyes. "Well, he couldn't ride two bikes, could he, dodo?" he says to his younger sister.

"Well then whoooo took it?" Morgan demands.

Coolly, I say, "George took it."

"GEORGE!" Morgan shouts.

I know she's thinking of her friend, not mine, but I just shrug. In seconds, Morgan has her phone out and is texting her friend George about stealing her bike. As she types she whispers, "What the heck, man?" I'll tell the truth later, if it comes up.

Smiling, I close my eyes.

CHAPTER 40
GEORGE

I peer through the zoo gates as Jack drives away with his family. We wave to each other the entire time. When the car becomes too tiny to see, my arm flops to my side. He's gone.

He said I matter, though. And I know he believed it. Which makes whatever happens to me next a little less scary.

I could follow him, but I don't. Jack needs to be with his family, and I need to get to know *my* new family. Clearly, I have some communication issues to work through with Wendla.

I reenter the zoo pavilion and sit on Jack's and my bench, where I can watch the people go by. Most rush past, eager to get to the next animal, but some stop and stare, and one or two even smile. I'm sure they're not actually looking at me, so I don't smile back. Instead my mind wanders to the adventures I just had with Jack and the ones I wish we'd had before we parted ways again.

The next thing I know, the worlds start to blend. There Jack and I are, walking across a tightrope over the bubbling lava of a volcano below. Here we are again, racing through the local grocery store to escape the pursuing pirates led by our archnemesis, Captain Sterling Silverstein, who has stolen the Great Macaroni's magic wand! With each new image, my grin gets wider and wider. Just as I'm picturing poor Uncle Chester as a damsel in distress, tied to a tree while Jack, Wanda, and I creep through the thick jungle foliage, a figure sits next to me on the bench.

I'm brought back to reality and am shocked to see—"Jack's dad?"

He looks straight ahead.

"I just wanted to thank you," he begins.

Me? What does he want to thank me for? I can't even imagine. I don't want to argue with a grown-up, so instead I just say, "You're welcome." He still hasn't looked at me, and to be honest, I'm not sure he's even talking to me, but there doesn't seem to be anyone else around.

"For helping Jack."

We sit side by side, neither one saying a word. Before I know it, my mind is off again. This time, Jack, the mysterious gopher lady, and I are swinging through the trees with some newfound monkey friends.

Jack's dad rises and crosses to the walrus exhibit. His hand rests on the top of the fence as he peers down. "Take care of George," he instructs my family below. His voice breaks as he adds, "For Jack." He pats the glass twice, and the next thing I know, Jack's dad is gone. I can't help but wonder if he was even here to begin with. I hoist myself off the bench and waddle toward Uncle Chester's exhibit.

There's a crinkle as I step. I reach into my pocket and pull out both halves of the runaway, torn, once-drenched and disintegrating, now hard and crusty poster. *Have you seen this person?*

Neither Jack nor I need this anymore. I proudly stride to the recycling bin, finally able to complete the task. It should be easy, but my hand clutches the sheet, hovering over the bin, refusing to let go.

I know Jack said I matter, but I still can't shake what he said about being real. Without Jack, I was invisible. But if I hadn't left Jack, I never would've found my family or learned I was magic at all. That was all me, and it's kind of amazing. Fantastic, if you ask the Great Macaroni! I found me. I was lucky.

But what about the others? The ones who flashed into my mind on the cartoon bus. The mop man. The gopher lady's sister. I'd be a fool if I didn't realize what they were. What I am.

I close my eyes and will myself to disappear one last time. When my eyelids peep open, the zoo is gone, replaced by the wiggly rainbow world of forgotten friends.

The brontosaurus in galoshes is still waiting on the street corner, afraid to cross.

A bus pulls up and stops right in front of me. The frazzled gopher sister, Miranda, exits, followed by my pal, Old Mopsy.

"George?" Old Mopsy says, rather stunned to see me. "In and out with this one," he tells Miranda, not even trying to sop up his jealousy.

I reach out and touch one of his floppy hands. It's soggy, which shouldn't surprise me, but it does. "You're fantastic," I tell him. "And I believe in you."

The place where his brow should be scrunches up, ringing out a bit of water. "What?" he asks, as he slowly fades from view, disappearing from this pretend rainbow world and returning to the real one, where he belongs.

I turn to Miranda. Her mouth falls open. Before she can even ask where Old Mopsy went, I say, "Your sister is something else."

She tilts her head.

"No, really," I say, so she doesn't confuse it for a compliment. "What is up with the bossing and the ballooning?" Miranda snorts. I reach out and touch her arm as well. "You're something else, too. And I believe in you." As she also evaporates, I call out, "Now go find your sister!" I hope she hears me. I hope she finds her.

I look at the dinosaur, almost about to take a step forward, his shaking leg hovering above the cross-walk. "I believe in you, too, Buster. That you can cross the street, and that you are a truly wonderful being." Slowly, I walk down the street, telling the talking houses and the flying mice and the four-headed barbershop quartet and everyone I see that they are wonderful. That they matter. And that I, George, will always believe in them.

One by one, they fade from view, until this rainbow world is a colorless void. My work is done. I close my eyes and again recall how much I matter, tapping my heels together three times for dramatic effect.

My heart jumps as I hear some kids laughing. I open my eyes and find myself back at the zoo. I notice a brontosaurus in rain boots making quite a stir with some kids near the reptile house. Over by the restroom, a janitor opens a supply closet door and grabs a mop. He yelps when the mop seems to grab him back. A smile spreads across my face. I did it.

Buster takes a liking to one particular girl, and they walk off together. I'm so excited for the fun they're going to have. It makes me remember all the fun Jack and I used to have.

Studying the poster, which is somehow still in my hands, a brilliant idea pops into my head, as if by magic. "Or should I say, the fun Jack and I *will* have," I murmur to myself, before dropping the poster into the recycling bin and dashing off to Uncle Chester's place so that the Great Georgini can perform his last, most amazing trick of all.

CHAPTER 41
JACK

Things can really change in just a week.

Mom and I are staying with Aunt Rachel and Uncle Dave while Mom gets the help she needs. I'm still sharing Jason's room, but now we have a bunk bed so I'll feel more at home. Mom explained that she has something called bipolar disorder. We're still talking about exactly what that means, but she says with medication and therapy, she's going to be okay. We're going to be okay. And this time, I really believe it.

When she's not in therapy, Mom spends a lot of her time fixing my hair and repeating, "I'm sorry, baby," and crying and begging me to forgive her.

"It's okay, Mom. I get it." Trying to show her how okay-ish I am, I brace myself and ask, "You want to tell me about that guy?" Teasing, I add, "Gavin, is it? Gustave? Gabriel?"

"It's Greg," she says with a laugh. "And he was a mistake. There's only one guy I need." She boops me on the nose like I'm not almost eleven, but I let her because she's right.

"For now," Aunt Rachel chimes in with a chuckle from the other room. I pretend not to hear this last part because she's still my mom, but when she's ready, I'll pretend to be ready, too.

Dad comes back for a visit, too, like he promised. He's all "I'm sorry, buddy!"—crying and begging me to forgive him almost as much as Mom.

I tell him I'll think about it, but that it is nice to see him again. I remind him that I'd like to see him more often. "Perhaps a trip to Daddy-O's?"

He looks puzzled but says, "Sure."

"And maybe you could bring your someone special," I offer with only a slight cringe.

"My *other* someone special," he corrects.

Jason and I have been playing a lot of duel-a-taire. Morgan even tried to play once. She has a lot more free time now that she and her friend George are fighting. They've both taught me a bunch more games too, and when we went outside to play football, Morgan actually chose me for her team first. Once.

I haven't heard from *my* George, but—

"Jack?"

Aunt Rachel walks into Jason's and my room holding a shoebox full of newspaper clippings.

"What's that?" I ask.

"Your mom told me about George," Aunt Rachel begins, taking a seat beside me on the bottom bunk.

I blush. "My George?" I ask, making sure she's talking about my best friend and that I'm not being busted for Morgan's fight with that other George.

"About your height? Mustache? Part walrus?" she confirms, smiling.

That's the guy. I grin back, surprised that Mom remembered those details, and for once even got the right species.

"I used to have a friend like him, too," she says. "Carmen." She pulls out a crayon drawing of a girl with her arm around a fuzzy-faced creature in an oversized hat. "She was part otter."

I laugh. That's ridiculous. I like it.

Aunt Rachel laughs too. "When I was about your age, I stopped . . ." she pauses. "Well, Carmen and I lost touch. But whenever I felt sad or angry or anything, I missed her like you wouldn't believe. I even started looking for her, and one day"—she points to an especially old-looking newspaper clipping—"I swear I saw her. In the background, but still, right there in the picture."

She hands me the paper. *Local Pie-Eating Contest Overrun by Rabbits*, the headline reads. The picture shows several hungry-looking people glaring at some hungrier-looking rabbits eating all the pies before them. And the smudge way in the background, behind it all—well, it does look kind of part-otter-y.

I blink and look again. Wait a second. That hat. That furry face.

"Could she balloonify herself?" I ask.

Aunt Rachel's mouth drops open. "How did you know?"

"'Part otter' could easily be mistaken for 'part gopher,'" I respond, as if that answers her question. "Carmen," I say softly to myself, nodding and smiling at the thought of George's friend and guardian, who tried so hard to help him and to bring me back to Rachel.

Aunt Rachel raises the box up and down to show how full it's become. "I got into the habit of looking for her, and I guess I've never stopped. The kids don't understand."

"I do," I say.

She smiles. "I thought you might." She pushes a stray strand of hair behind her ear. "Anyway," she says, "I just thought I'd tell you he's never gone. You just need to know where to look." She stands up. "Maybe you could hold on to this for a bit?" she asks, patting the box. "Look through it. Add your own?"

I nod.

She turns to leave the room but stops. "Oh, I almost forgot," she adds. Pulling an envelope out of her back pocket, she drops it into my hands. "Mail."

"Mail?" I ask, more than a little surprised.

She shrugs before leaving the room. "Dinner's at six," she calls over her shoulder. "Your mom'll be back from therapy by then."

Alone in the bedroom, I turn the envelope over in my hands. On the front it says *Jack*. I recognize George's handwriting at once. Quickly I run my finger through the envelope, tearing it open.

I pull out the single sheet and unfold it.

Dear Jack, it begins. I smile. It's good to hear his voice.

How are you? I'm good. Living with my Uncle Chester and his good friends Wanda and Wendla has been really nice. Wendla's sorry about scaring you. She thought you were a treat. When I told her all about you, she said she guesses you ARE a treat, but not the kind you eat. She's funny, right?

I've been going on a lot of adventures that you wouldn't even believe! And you were right. I've made a lot of new friends here. There's Weatherby. He's a security guard penguin, and get this—he can hold his breath for SIX whole days when dared. There's Old Mopsy, who helps the custodian. Buster the brontosaurus promised I could visit his new friend Aileen. Even the terrifying gopher lady isn't so bad. Did you know she has a twin? You should see them together.

Oh! And I haven't told you the greatest news of all: I have a new BEST friend! He's really nice. Very funny. He loves the jokes you've told me. I've shared them all with him. I didn't think you'd mind. In fact I think you'd get along with him really well if you ever happened to meet him. He's actually a lot like you. His name is Jack, and I imagined him myself! My greatest trick yet.

I hope you're doing well. Your cards are mainly dry now, and New Jack and I are taking good care of them. I sent you this one to help you remember me. Please do, because I will never forget you.

Love, your very best friend,
George

I reach into the envelope and pull out the card. It's the Jack of Hearts.

I grin.

I slide the card and the letter back into the envelope, before carefully placing it inside the box on top of Aunt Rachel's scraps. Getting up, I take the box to the dresser drawer that's been set aside for me. I peek at the blank sheet inside the envelope one last time before wedging the box between my clothes in the bottom drawer.

Making my way back to the bed, I sit down and wait. Wait for dinner. For Jason to challenge me to a game of duel-a-taire.

Wait for Mom to get here. To get better.

Wait for Daddy-O's with Dad.

Wait for whatever it is my best friend George imagines me doing next.

ACKNOWLEDGMENTS

Jack and George's story began thirteen years ago as a writing exercise in my first class at Simmons College, taught by the amazingly talented Jo Knowles. Jo has continued to encourage and inspire me over the years. This book would have never sprouted without you, Jo. I am so grateful to call you a mentor and a friend.

I received my first critique on this manuscript from my classmates—Sandy, Kathy, Shoshana, Mary Ellen, Emily, Dani, Melissa, Brittany, and Jennifer. Thank you for your early notes and support. I have so much love and respect for all of you, and I cannot wait to see your works out in the world one day. A special thanks to the rest of the faculty and students at Simmons, especially Cathryn Mercier, Anna Staniszewski, and Susan Bloom <3, from whom I learned so much.

This story would not be what it is today without so many friends and readers who were able to offer their insight along the way. Thank you to everyone who has ever read a draft or an excerpt and helped me see things in a different light: Janet, Carter, Esther, Stephanie, Ariel, Sylvie, Hilary, Jen, Amanda, Rob, Andrew, Ben, Sarah, and so many more. Aileen—thank you for Buster. Jen, thank you for letting me take the time off of work to complete the final revisions.

Paige, your particular notes for this project were invaluable. Thank you for initiating the Old Mopsy/Jason fan clubs. Dawn, thank you for keeping me accountable and for inspiring me to keep going. Courtney and Marie, thank you for always being willing to interrupt our regularly scheduled chatting to answer my hundreds of tiny questions about grammar and for reassuring me every step of the way.

To my amazing agent, Emily Keyes, you inspired the revision that finally made this story click. The best parts of this book exist because of your notes and feedback, and I cannot thank you enough. I still cannot believe how lucky I am to work with you. Thank you for answering all my panicked questions, for keeping me (relatively) calm throughout this terrifyingly exciting process, and for caring so much about my characters. I promise you George eventually got his nachos. Thank you also to Laurie McLean and the rest of the team at Fuse Literary.

I'm so fortunate to have an amazing editor, Amy Fitzgerald. I'm so honored you saw the potential in Jack and George's journey, and were able to help further shape it into the story it is today. Your questions generated some of the scenes I am now proudest of. Thank you also to everyone at Lerner/Carolrhoda who played a part in the production of this book, including cover artist Tania Rex, designer Lindsey Owens, creative director Danielle Carnito, and production manager Erica Johnson. The cover and book design are gorgeous and have brought more life to this story than I could have ever imagined. To copyeditor Mahogony Francis and proofreader Jun Kuromiya, thank you for making it seem like I know what I'm doing. To Jo Knowles, Melissa D. Savage, Anna Staniszewski, thank you so much for your early reads and kind words.

To my in-laws and extended family, thank you for providing so much love. A special acknowledgment to my nieces and nephew: Natalie, Keira, Norah, Caleigh, and Andrew. I am so proud to be your uncle.

Thank you, Mom and Dad, for always encouraging my creative endeavors and for making me the person that I am today. I am also very fortunate to have four amazing siblings, whose support I could not manage without. Megan, Michael, Robert, and Brian, thank you for everything.

I need to send the most special of shout-outs to my best little friend, Rudy, who slept by my side for so much of this process. I hope the book is not as boring as your sleeping implies. You are the greatest dog, and you deserve all of the treats.

Scott, I do not even know how to thank you for everything. You have read this book more times than I have. This story is as much yours as it is mine. Thank you for each "I've changed these two sentences. Can you reread the entire book and tell me which version is better?" You are the George to my Jack. I cannot believe how lucky I am that you're both real and really mine.

Finally, to my readers, I am so honored and thankful you went on this journey with Jack and George. To everyone who is struggling with mental health issues, everyone who feels like they don't belong, everyone who has ever felt invisible, never be afraid to ask for help. You are real, you are part magic, and you deserve to be seen. I believe in you.

TOPICS FOR DISCUSSION

1. Why does Jack want to find George again?

2. Why do you think George is disappearing?

3. How has George changed since he left Jack? How is Jack different than he was when George last saw him?

4. How does Jack's mom's bipolar disorder affect her behavior? How does this make her actions different from Jack's dad's actions?

5. How do Jack's aunt, uncle, and step-cousins show that they care about him?

6. Jack fears that he's "just like Mom and Dad" because he's taken George for granted and "abandoned" him. Do you think he's right? Why or why not?

7. Jack and George both fear what will happen if Jack stops believing in George. How do they each learn to believe in themselves during the story?

8. Which of George's actions can be explained as things Jack actually did? Which things does he do that Jack couldn't have done?

9. How does George free the creatures in the rainbow-world and allow them to return to the real world? What does this tell you about George?

10. When Jack leaves the zoo for the last time, he waves goodbye to his dad. From George's point of view, Jack is waving goodbye to *him*. How are these two points of view about the same moment similar? How are they different?

11. Why do you think Jack and George are finally able to let go of each other?

12. What adventures do you think George will have next? What about Jack?

ABOUT THE AUTHOR

Jimmy Matejek–Morris grew up in New Jersey as the middle child of five kids. He enjoys musical theater, Muppets, ice cream, and action figures. His favorite activity is excitedly pointing out every animal he sees only to disappointedly realize that sometimes what looks like an armadillo in a top hat is just a plastic bag. He currently lives in Cambridge, Massachusetts with his husband, Scott, and a very well-dressed poodle-Pomeranian named Rudy. *My Ex-Imaginary Friend* is his debut novel.